He pressed hi
laced his fing
small of her ba
was a wall of v

'It doesn't make sense for you to protest, and push, and put up barriers, when I can feel how much we both want this. When I can feel that there's a spark, a magic, that I haven't felt in a long time, that I haven't ever felt quite the same as this,' he said.

'If you're looking for an affair…' She looked searchingly into his face.

'I'm not looking for an affair. Not just an affair, certainly. It's a starting point. We can take it very slowly, if you like. And we're free to stop it, either of us, if isn't working out.'

'I'm stopping it now, in that case.'

'No, you're not. Not until you tell me why.'

She sighed. 'This feels so…back to front.' She looked at him and saw how intently he was watching her. 'I have to tell you something. Far too soon. I know it's too soon. But I have to tell you. I'll just say it.'

'Go ahead.'

'I probably…more than probably…can't have children, Gian.'

Medical Romance™ is proud to present
an emotionally gripping duet by talented author

Lilian Darcy

Katherine and Emma are midwives
at a busy maternity unit in
GLENFALLON HOSPITAL.

Glenfallon is a large rural community
in the beautiful wine-making region of
New South Wales, Australia.

Don't miss Emma's story, coming in December 2003,
only in Medical Romance™.

And later, in 2004, look out for more
Glenfallon Hospital stories!

THE MIDWIFE'S COURAGE

BY
LILIAN DARCY

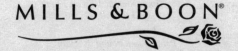

MILLS & BOON®

All the characters in this book have no existence outside the imagination of the author, and have no relation whatsoever to anyone bearing the same name or names. They are not even distantly inspired by any individual known or unknown to the author, and all the incidents are pure invention.

*First published in Great Britain 2003
Harlequin Mills & Boon Limited,
Eton House, 18-24 Paradise Road, Richmond, Surrey TW9 1SR*

© Lilian Darcy 2003

ISBN 0 263 83481 6

*Set in Times Roman 10½ on 12 pt.
03-1103-50531*

*Printed and bound in Spain
by Litografía Rosés, S.A., Barcelona*

CHAPTER ONE

WITHIN a few days, the farm felt like home to Katherine McConnell.

Her decision to come and live here with Aunt Helen was a problem solver for both of them. At sixty, Helen had been finding the farm difficult to manage since Uncle Brian's death last year.

'Mentally more than physically,' she'd said, on the day Kit had arrived, with tears welling in her kind blue eyes. Kit knew they'd had a good marriage, as did her own parents, now running a retail business in Queensland. Aunt Helen was her father's sister. 'It will be wonderful to have you here, Kit!'

Talking about it, they'd touched far less on Kit's own reasons for making the move, although Aunt Helen knew the basic facts about her drawn-out break-up with James. That they'd been having problems for a while. That James had found someone else.

Aunt Helen didn't know the underlying source of those problems, however.

Kit had reached breaking point the day she found out that James's new partner, Tammy, was planning to have her pre-natal care and her delivery in Kit's own maternity department at Canberra's Black Mountain Hospital. Kit had picked up the manila file folder containing Tammy's notes and barged into the next office, her competence and control hanging by a fragile thread.

'I can't see this next patient, Rosemary!' she'd said to

the other midwife taking appointments at that morning's clinic. 'I just can't!'

She'd resigned the following week, desperately in need of a change.

Now, three difficult months later, she was here.

Closing the gate behind her car, so that the sheep wouldn't stray into the yard from their nearby paddock, Kit paused for a few moments, purely to appreciate her new surroundings.

It was early afternoon, and a colony of sulphur-crested cockatoos was squabbling up in the big eucalyptus trees by the creek. The hens were strutting about their run, poking their beaks at kitchen scraps and grain. Kit had collected seven eggs first thing this morning, and had eaten two of them for breakfast, relishing the fresh taste of the thick, golden yolks.

A line of old pepper trees ran along the fence, shading it with their frond-like leaves. Kit picked a handful of the dusky pink, paper-skinned corns, breathed in their spicy fragrance then let them trickle through her fingers to the ground. One of the farm cats, a black and white neutered tom named Sid, padded up to her on his silent, fastidious paws and sniffed her legs.

In the distance, there were rolling yellow wheatfields and sheep paddocks, and just out of view on the flatter and more fertile land closer to the river, the brighter greens of vine-yards and citrus groves. The rocky hills were hazed with blue, and there came the faint sound of a tractor. Just the smell of the air was a balm to her spirits. A breeze lifted some strands of hair from her neck, and the sun shone on her back.

She'd spent the morning grocery shopping and running errands in town, before grabbing a quick lunch at the Glenfallon Bakery Café, in Glenfallon's main street. She would be starting her first shift at the hospital in an hour, which meant that there was time for a cup of tea at home before she changed into her uniform and left for work.

An unfamiliar car was already parked on the grass in the shade of the pepper trees. Aunt Helen had company, Kit realised. Gathering several bags of groceries in her arms, she went into the kitchen. The squeak and bang of the screen door announced her arrival, but Helen and her visitor must have heard the car a minute or two earlier as well.

They were through in the sitting room, basking in a shaft of warm autumn sun that fell across the twin armchairs. Putting down the groceries and starting to unpack, Kit caught a glimpse of an older woman, who was moving her hands expressively in the air as she spoke.

'I can't understand a woman not wanting children but, there, that's my prejudice, I know. The point is, Gian wanted them, and that's an incompatibility you can't get around, can you? Gian was willing to live in Sydney, but that wasn't much use when they couldn't agree on the question of a family. It's already more than a year since their divorce was finalised.'

'Life was simpler, in some ways, when we were young, wasn't it?' Aunt Helen agreed. 'We had fewer choices!' Then she raised her voice. 'Kit?'

'Just unpacking the shopping,' Kit called back.

'Don't. Come and have a cuppa with us instead.'

Further persuasion was not required. Kit grabbed a nice big mug from the draining basket and went through.

'Freddie, this is my niece Katherine, whom we always call Kit,' Aunt Helen said. 'Kit, this is Federica Di Luzio, our neighbour a couple of kilometres down the road.'

'Oh, the vineyard?'

'Yes, only I can't take any credit for those rows of green vines marching across the landscape.' The older woman smiled. 'All our land is leased out to the Glen Aran winery, across the road, now. It's so nice for Helen that you've come, Kit.'

'Not a bad deal for me either,' she said laughing, as Aunt Helen filled her mug with dark, strong tea. 'I've always loved this farm.'

'You'll meet Gian, my son, too,' Federica went on. 'Helen has told me you're starting at the hospital today. He's Dr Di Luzio, and he looks very much like me.'

Really? It seemed unlikely, to Kit.

Federica Di Luzio was round and warm and maternal-looking, and only about five feet three. Her hair was tinted an attractive light brown, growing out just perceptibly at the roots to show the grey, and her olive skin, although lined, was fine-pored and smooth. She had dark brown eyes and wore no make-up, but even thus unadorned it was impossible to imagine a masculine version of her face.

'I must go,' she said now. 'Bonnie has been at a little friend's house for lunch, and she'll need an afternoon sleep soon.' Her eyes warmed, and she smiled again.

'You're brave to have taken it on, Freddie,' Aunt Helen told her, but Mrs Di Luzio only laughed.

'It keeps me out of trouble, and it gives me someone to hug. Gian won't let me do that to him too often! Anyway, was there a choice? She's flesh and blood, and I love her to pieces.'

'I still think you should be proud of yourself.'

The two women went out to the yard, still talking, and Kit took her half-drunk tea into the kitchen and went on unpacking the groceries. A few minutes later, Helen came back inside.

'Isn't she lovely, Kit? We hadn't caught up for ages, what with one thing and another, but we've resolved to do better from now on. I hadn't realised until—until Brian died how much I'd need my female friends.'

'From the little I saw of her, she seems terrific,' Kit agreed gently. Aunt Helen had turned away, to stare blindly down into the kitchen sink. 'Great to have compatible neighbours.'

Kit's aunt lifted her head again, and some brightness crept back into her tone. 'She has her little granddaughter to care for—permanently, it looks like. Bonnie's a handful. It must be hard at Freddie's age, even though she shrugs off that idea. She's two years older than I am.' Aunt Helen was sixty. 'She takes it in her stride wonderfully.'

'What happened to the parents?'

'Her other son is in Hong Kong. Never met his little girl until she was several months old. The mother was a difficult character, as I understand it, and the relationship didn't last long. She died of an overdose, and there was no one to take the baby, apart from Marco. But he was, well, ambivalent, apparently. Gob-smacked. Not ready to be a parent. And Freddie didn't want him to have to downgrade his career, or for the baby to be brought up by a nanny in a Hong Kong high-rise. I admire her tremendously. I'm not sure I could have done it.'

'You would, if the situation arose,' Kit told her. Kit's two cousins were both happily married. Sandra lived on another farm about half an hour's drive away, which allowed her husband Mike to help Helen with the heavy work around this place, while Chris worked for the government in Canberra.

'I wouldn't look as fresh and cheerful as Federica does,' Helen answered. 'Stop doing that,' she added. Kit was still putting groceries away. 'Let me finish.'

'I will, because it's time to change,' Kit said, hiding a faint sense of trepidation.

It was a long time since she'd experienced that First Day feeling.

Gian Di Luzio arrived at the hospital with his mind on the surgery he was about to perform. It was a Caesarean delivery of twins, with the larger of the babies in a frank breech position. The baby had been that way when Gian had last checked, and the midwife in the maternity unit had confirmed the same position fifteen minutes ago, when she examined the patient.

Mrs Frampton had been scheduled for a Caesarean the following week if the breech baby's position hadn't changed, but Gian wasn't surprised that she'd jumped the gun. Twins very often came early. This time, Mrs Frampton's waters had broken in the middle of the supermarket, and labour had started almost at once. Gian wanted to get these babies out before the pressure of the contractions pushed that little rear end too tightly down into the birth canal.

He jerked to a halt in one of the reserved spaces next to the entrance to the maternity wing just as another car scraped its tyres against the kerb. Two women got out at the same time as he did, and they immediately began to help a third, who was heavily pregnant and obviously in labour.

'I can't!' he heard.

'You can! You're almost there, then we'll have help on hand. Not that we'll need it, because you're doing so great, Laurel.'

'It's been more than two days…'

'It hasn't. Not really. It only feels that way. You started slowly, that's all.'

Moving faster than the trio of women, Gian ducked

ahead of them. They weren't his business. Or at any rate, not yet. The automatic doors slid open and he went inside.

Sister Emma Burns pounced on him the moment he entered the unit, one level up. 'Things are hotting up fast. How's your breech technique, Dr Di Luzio?'

'Rusty, but we're not going to test it. Is Clive here?'

'Just about.' Emma nodded over Gian's shoulder and he turned to find the anaesthetist right behind him, a little breathless.

'Good!' Gian said. 'Meanwhile, you've got another customer, Sister Burns, and she'll need some attention. She's got friends bringing her up from the car, and she's exhausted. Get an accurate handle on how long she's actually been in labour, and…not to tell you your job—'

'Tell me my job, Dr Di Luzio, I can take it.'

'Check the baby's condition.'

'We generally do,' she drawled.

'Hmm,' was all Gian said.

He had conservative instincts on these matters, and he knew it. He could have blamed his even more conservative training in Sydney, but that wouldn't quite have been fair. The conservatism came from within himself, and his sense of where certain priorities should fall. He rubbed the nursing staff up the wrong way sometimes, but usually managed to deflect any real conflict through humour and a willingness to compromise.

Heading with long strides towards the almost-new obstetric operating theatre he'd christened with its first procedure just a few weeks ago, Gian caught a glimpse of the midwife who was replacing Jean Darby.

Bless Jean! he thought. May she enjoy a very satisfactory retirement!

This new one was young and blonde-streaked and slim. She had her hair cut short and feathery, and she had beautiful ivory skin in contrast to her brown eyes. If he'd heard her name at any point, he didn't remember it.

He didn't have time to see any more of her than this one brief glimpse, but heard Emma Burns behind him saying to her, 'Ready for your first? Dr Di Luzio suggests that we…'

The sound of running water hitting the bottom of the big stainless-steel sink, as he began to scrub, drowned out the rest of her words.

Clive worked quickly, and Mrs Frampton was soon well under anaesthesia. Within a minute or two, Gian had incised his way through the outer layers of skin and muscle, and breached the wall of the uterus. He removed the baby girl first, slippery and wet. She was the smaller of the two. Would weigh just a little over two kilograms, at his best guess, and might need some extra attention during her first few days of life.

Midwife Jane Cameron suctioned her mouth and nose quickly, and cut and clamped the cord. The baby gave her first satisfying cry, and healthy pink began to radiate outwards from torso to bluish extremities.

The boy was next, and required some deft yet firm manoeuvring to slide him free of the pelvis. He looked as if he would weigh close to a kilogram more than the baby girl, and Gian teased him softly, 'Been starving your sister, little man?'

He cried at once, his open mouth huge in his little screwed-up face, and his wet black hair like a silky wig, incongruous on such a tiny head. Over the next few weeks, Mrs Frampton would get tired of the repeated comment, 'Hasn't he got a lot of hair!'

With less haste and more deliberation, Gian delivered the two placentas and made sure they were complete. As he would have expected, given their differing birth weights, the placenta which had nourished the boy was the heavier of the two. Next, he began to close the incision.

Around him, the familiar routine of surgery continued to unfold. The babies were wheeled to the side of the room in their special cribs. Their five-minute Apgar scores were eight and nine respectively, giving a good prognosis for their future. The nurses counted through their equipment and confirmed that nothing was missing. Clive Alderson gave a running commentary on where he and the patient were up to.

Gian pulled off his gloves within forty minutes of parking the car. He was satisfied with the result and looked forward to seeing the mother with her new twins later on, when he visited their room.

Passing the nurses' station, he asked Emma, 'How's your latest baby?'

'Never mind that for the moment. How are yours? I know Mrs Frampton was worried about one of them being breech.'

'I asked first, Sister Burns.'

Emma sighed. And smiled. She was a nice woman, around thirty-three or thirty-four, with a mass of dark hair, severe eyebrows and brown eyes. She was prettier than she looked. That didn't exactly make sense, but it was true, all the same. And she was much put upon, Gian understood, by a difficult stepmother. She'd inherited the woman, so to speak, when her father died, and apparently no one else wanted her.

'The baby is fine,' she said. 'Kit McConnell, our new recruit, listened to the heartbeat and it was good and strong.'

'Between contractions, or during? Did she do an internal?' Emma opened her mouth to reply, but he cut her off.

'I know the policy on internal examinations. Only if the mother wants one. Quite often, they do.'

'She didn't.'

'*She* didn't, or her friends? And how long since true labour began?'

It sounded as if he was attacking Sister Burns, he realised. She was handling it calmly, but he backed off all the same, and said in a neutral tone, 'Never mind. I'll take a look. My problem, OK? Just something I overheard down by the car, and I want to check it out. People aren't always accurate. Or honest.'

The explanation didn't make much sense, but he left her to deal with it anyway. Remembered to throw back over his shoulder, 'The twins are going to be fine, by the way. Girl is a little small. Might be in Special Care for a day or two. The boy's a bruiser.'

'Room Two, Dr Di Luzio.'

'Thanks.'

He collided with the new midwife—Kit something—right in the doorway, ended up with a hand cupping her elbow and her toe pressuring his foot. He smelled lilac and peaches and the starchy, synthetic smell of new uniform. He had time to notice that her lovely, fine-pored skin was stretched over smooth arms and a very graceful neck.

'Oops,' she gasped. She looked preoccupied.

'Problem?' He navigated her by the elbow back out the door, and spoke quietly.

She looked up into his face. Her almond-shaped brown eyes were fringed with thick lashes and, at the moment, shadowed by a worried frown. And there was something about her mouth, about the fullness of her upper lip, that spoke volumes. He sensed that she had a good bit of history behind that pretty face.

'The heart rate has dropped,' she said. 'Pretty suddenly.

It's down to seventy beats a minute during contractions, and barely coming back up between them. I'm not sure what's going on. The patient says she's only been in labour since last night, but she's exhausted. I don't like the pressure her friends are putting on her. There's a border-line between encouragement and bullying, and I feel they're on the wrong side of it. There's some mec. staining, too.'

'How dilated is she?'

'Well, the policy in this unit—'

'For heaven's sake, I know the policy in this unit!' Gian said, and muttered an oath.

He pushed impatiently past the new midwife, back into the room, keeping his distance from her personal space. There was still a faint aura of sensation...and scent...and warmth...clinging to him from when they'd collided, but he paid it no attention. There were far more important issues uppermost in his mind.

The patient's two labour partners looked up at him at once—defiantly, to his critical gaze.

'I want to take a closer look at what's going on, Laurel,' he said to the patient herself. Kept his tone brisk and cheerful.

She gave him an exhausted, agonised glance and didn't speak. A contraction began, hard on the heels of the one before, and she puffed raggedly through it, gripping her friends' arms, breaking off to moan. Her control lay in fragments, and her body was bathed in sweat.

'She's doing fine,' one of the women said.

Gian didn't waste time on questioning his own preconceptions. Whatever the ramifications of the relationship between the three, whatever was signified by the absence of a father, it wasn't his concern.

'But the baby might need some help,' he answered gently, hiding his anger. 'The heart rate is low, and the waters aren't clear. Laurel, I want to check you out, and the baby, and I want you to prepare yourself for what's probably going to end up as an emergency Caesarean.'

'She doesn't want that sort of intervention,' one of her supporters said.

Gian ignored her. 'Laurel, I need to hear from you on this.'

'I don't care...any more,' she gasped.

Gian was already listening to the baby. Seventy beats a minute, Kit McConnell had said. Now it was lower. Erratic, too, and not strong.

'Get Clive,' he said urgently, then remembered that this peach-and-lilac midwife with history in her face was new. 'Anaesthetist. She'll need a general. No time for epidural. They'll still be clearing up in the ob theatre. This can't wait. We'll go down to the main theatre suite. And can you—?'

'Hang on a minute, Dr Whoever-you-are!' The more vocal of the supporters again.

'Di Luzio. Gian Di Luzio,' he supplied, terse now.

'This is Laurel's birth process. Aren't you going to consult—?'

There was no sense in losing control, although Gian came close. He said very deliberately and carefully, 'This isn't about Laurel now, I'm afraid. It's about the baby. Which may have serious problems if labour drags on any longer. When did it start?'

Kit slipped past him, out of the room, as he asked the question. Her hips moved with the grace of a dancer, but her shoulders looked surprisingly square and sturdy. The combination of delicacy and strength that she gave off was unusual.

'She was having contractions on Saturday, but—' one of the women began defensively.

'No. Friday,' Laurel gasped.

'Three *days* ago?'

'They weren't intense,' said the second supporter. 'Not really. And they began quite far apart. About thirty minutes for the first couple of hours, and then—'

'Regular? Increasing in frequency and duration? Painful?'

'Yes, but she could breathe through them quite comfortably until—'

Emma appeared in the doorway, her dark frown emphasising the habitual brooding look on her face. 'Clive's on his way down. Julie will circulate, and Kit's going to scrub. But Special Care is short-staffed today, and with the little Frampton girl needing some—'

'Try Pete Croft or Alison Cairns, whoever's closest on hand,' Gian told her. 'I want to get this baby out within the next ten minutes.'

'Patriarchal pig,' came a muttered voice in the background.

'Arrogant bloody creep!' said a second voice.

The hair on the back of Gian's neck began to prickle and he swore. The obscenity—moderate word, strong tone— caught Kit like a slap on her ivory-and-peaches cheek as she appeared again. He hadn't intended that, but he *was* angry with her. With everyone, in fact, himself included. This shouldn't be happening.

'We have an orderly on the way,' she said, then added quickly and quietly, 'Dr Di Luzio, I realise you must want me to go on ahead, but I'm not sure where the theatre suite is, and I don't want—'

'Oh, great!' came the 'patriarchal pig' voice.

'Come on,' Gian told her, gripping her elbow and pulling her with him. 'You won't get lost with me.'

Walking beside him in a thick silence, Kit had to conclude inwardly, The man is nothing whatsoever like his mother!

Not in looks, and certainly not in temperament. Replace maternal brown eyes with diamond-hard black ones, add, oh, around a third of a metre of height, change a soft, wide smile to anger-thinned lips and concede that, before she went grey, Federica Di Luzio probably had hair as thick and dark and glossy as her son's.

And, OK, maybe their noses were the same, both of them straight and patrician like the noses of marble busts made in ancient Rome. An arrogant nose, in his case, shadowing an angry mouth.

End of resemblance.

Kit's heart thumped with sick-making abruptness in her chest. Dr Di Luzio unsettled her, made her as jumpy as a cat. She knew he had reason to be angry at the labouring woman's strident supporters, but it seemed as if he had plenty of anger left over for her as well. Her decisions. Her priorities. Her adherence to policy. The fact that she hadn't probed more deeply into the women's definition of 'labour'.

Emma had said, 'Get a clear history. Dr Di Luzio overheard something and thinks there's cause for concern.'

Kit had agreed, after ten minutes spent with the patient, that her supporters were hindering rather than helping, but they'd been quite firm on one point. 'Labour, proper labour, as defined in all the reading we did, didn't start until last night.'

Laurel herself had confirmed it. Laurel herself had gasped, 'No, I don't want an internal exam, or an internal monitor. I'll know when it's time to push, right? Has to be soon…' But apparently the obstetrician's more detailed probing had yielded a changed story. Labour had actually begun three days ago.

What if the baby wasn't all right?

'Here we are,' Dr Di Luzio said. His voice was deep, and rich in tone.

Plunging into the familiar routine of a Caesarean delivery, albeit an urgent one, acted as a calming blanket on Kit's jangled nerves. They prepped the equipment, prepped the patient, adjusted the lights. Dr Di Luzio didn't waste a word. The baby was out a minute and a half before his darkly threatened deadline, and into the hands of the doctor who'd been called in.

It was a girl. She was limp and unresponsive, and smeared with meconium. The fact that she wasn't breathing on her own was, for the moment, a plus. It bought the doctor and nurse who were working over her a crucial interval of time in which to suction her nose and mouth so that when she did breathe, she didn't inhale the dark, sticky and potentially fatal faecal matter.

'Airway clear now,' the doctor muttered, after the seconds had dragged on. Kit had caught his name at one point, but had forgotten it. Pete, maybe? 'She's a bit shocked. I'm going to bag her.'

'You want the pulse oximeter in place?'

'Yes, please, Vanessa.'

'One-minute Apgar score—five,' the nurse said.

'The five-minute score is the one that really counts.'

'Let's hope we got to her in time,' Gian muttered wearily, and turned his attention at last to the patient's incision.

His hands were as expressive as his mother's, Kit conceded. They moved with angular and angry precision, never rough but very crisp and fast. He worked as quickly and neatly as the best obstetricians she'd seen in Canberra and Sydney, but there was no small talk, and over in the far corner, the doctor and nurse were frowning over the little girl.

In desperation, hating the atmosphere and the pervasive

sense that the baby might not be all right, Kit asked the obstetrician quietly, 'What should I have done differently, Dr Di Luzio? How could I have stopped this from…?' She stopped, and began again, determined to get this right, so that their working relationship wasn't ruined from the beginning. 'I'm not challenging your perspective. I just want to know what you think.'

'You think it's you I'm angry with,' he muttered, drawing the two sides of the incision together.

'Yes. Aren't you? Partly, at least. I don't imagine being labelled a patriarchal pig and an arrogant creep helped your mood.'

'I've heard worse.' He interrupted himself. 'Julie, can you—? The black, yes. Thanks.' He added to Kit, 'It really doesn't matter.'

'To be called names?'

'To be disliked. Feared, even. If it gets results.'

'Do we go back half a century, then, Dr Di Luzio?' Julie asked. 'With rigid hierarchy, and nurses treated like ignorant maidservants?'

Pete and Vanessa worked on the baby. Clive minded his own business. The debate took place between Gian and the two midwives.

'Sometimes,' the obstetrician answered as he worked. 'If that yields the outcome we want. I think we're too hung up on the mother having a good birth experience. Sorry. I'm conservative on that. I'm sceptical about home births, and water births, and labours that aren't fully monitored. The outcome I want is a healthy baby, and if the atmosphere isn't rosy around the edges, so be it. We may not have achieved the right goal today. This baby may not be all right.'

'Because I didn't push harder?' Kit watched another suture slip neatly into position.

She was pushing now. Pushing him, although she didn't enjoy doing it. She would have to work with this man, however. It wasn't the time to be timid.

'And because I didn't,' he answered her. 'Because I didn't communicate well enough with Emma, and because Emma didn't communicate well enough with you. Because the mother, bullied by her friends, was putting the birth experience ahead of the baby. We're all at fault.'

'Looking much better, everybody,' Pete said. 'Spontaneous respiration happening now. Five-minute Apgar score is eight.'

'Eight?' Dr Di Luzio repeated. 'Couldn't hope for better than that.'

'Considering how she looked when she came out, yes.' The highest possible Apgar score was ten. 'And she's opened her eyes. She's looking at me. She's got her fist in her mouth and she's sucking it. Hear?' They all could, a strong, slurping, rhythmic sound. 'We may have a winner here after all.'

Kit blinked back hot tears of relief, and watched as Gian's hands stilled for a moment over the patient's flaccid, half-stitched lower abdomen. Glancing up, she saw that he'd momentarily closed his eyes above his mask. The stillness in his face emphasised his classic bone structure—smooth forehead, confident jaw, symmetrical cheekbones. She felt a little lurch in her stomach that she couldn't explain, an awakening of something inside her that she'd feared was gone forever.

When he opened his eyes again, she caught a glimpse of the same expression that had been on Federica Di Luzio's face earlier this afternoon, when she'd talked about her granddaughter.

Ten minutes later, she saw him approach Laurel's two

friends. They were pacing the corridor outside the theatre suite, wearing expressions creased with concern.

'Laurel has a beautiful baby girl,' he said to them. 'She'll spend some time in the special care unit until we can see how she's doing. And Laurel is in Recovery. You should be able to see her soon. Any questions, please, ask.'

Much later, after her evening meal break, Kit felt a substantial presence leaning across the desk at the nurses' station where she was working. She looked up.

'That wasn't a great introduction for you, today,' Gian said. 'I want to apologise for contributing to it.'

'I understood what you were saying,' she answered, taking her hand from the smooth plastic shape of the computer mouse and curving it around her knee, just where the fabric of her blue surgical gear stretched tight. She was conscious of him, now, in a way that was unsettling—conscious of his bulk, his dark colouring, his instinctive aura of presence and confidence. 'If you saw more of the really wonderful, relaxed, easy births that the nursing staff so often deal with…'

'I have seen those,' he pointed out. 'Plenty of times, during my training. I still see them, with private patients, or when problems we've anticipated don't actually occur. I don't try to turn every woman's delivery into a technological nightmare.'

'But a technological miracle…?'

'Yes. It's worth more than some people think.'

They smiled at each other. Cautiously. He added, 'My mother tells me we're neighbours, at a distance of two kilometres.'

'Oh, you live on the farm with her?'

'No, I have a unit here in town, a couple of streets away. But the farm has always felt like home, and since my little niece came along, I'm spending more time there. Mum needs the help with Bonnie, although she's having trouble accepting that.'

'She's pretty good, isn't she? I liked her.'

'She has her moments!'

They smiled again.

Dr Di Luzio was wearing a suit now, and had obviously come in to check on his patients before going out to dinner, or perhaps a meeting. He looked impressive, attractive and very European with his dark colouring. If Kit had never heard him speak before, she might have expected an accent, but even Federica didn't have one. The family must have been in Australia for a while.

Still, there was a cultural heritage. Instinctively, as she looked at him, Kit thought not of harsh operating lights and the glare of surgical instruments, or even of a stethoscope pressed questingly to a woman's warm, swollen belly in search of the sound of a heartbeat, but of far more sensual things. Heat rising from soil, the warm smell of fresh-picked summer fruits and the richness of wine.

She realised, too late, that she must have been staring at him far too openly. His next words flustered her still further.

'Listen, I wanted to make you welcome here, especially after today,' he said. 'Would you like to grab a meal later in the week? Which nights are you free?'

Kit wasn't sure if she wanted to go. He was being neighbourly—and 'welcoming', as he'd said. Possibly his mother had put him up to it. With her recently developed instinct for self-preservation, she made light of the invitation.

'I'm more than happy to let you off with the apology you've already given, Dr Di Luzio,' she said.

He laughed. 'That's what you think? This was another apology? It's not.'

'Then it's your mother.'

'Not that either, although I recognise it's a plausible scenario. She's Italian enough to claim the right to meddle deeply in my personal life.' His smile was wicked, softening his black eyes into liquid pools. 'Most of the time, I don't let her.'

He paused, obviously waiting for her answer. Kit took a deep breath, but no words issued forth.

'You're running out of excuses,' Gian said softly. 'I can tell.'

And she had to laugh. 'A meal would be nice,' she conceded. 'I feel like I know the town, since I've been here for holidays as a child, but the town doesn't know me.'

'I'll…uh…invite some other people, start getting you known around here. I'm sorry, I should have made it clear straight away that's what I was thinking of.'

'I'd like that,' she told him truthfully.

Better than staring across a tiny table at a man she hardly knew, while they racked their brains for small talk.

It was a long time since she'd been out with a man. Well, with a man who wasn't James. She'd turned thirty-three at her last birthday, and she and James had been involved…had lived together…for six years.

'Friday?' Gian suggested, as he studied the shifting emotions reflected on Kit's expressive, sweet and history-laden face.

He wasn't sure if he was glad or sorry that he'd called in at the farm for an hour, late this afternoon. Mum loved to impart the details of other people's lives. Never maliciously. Always with the best of intentions. Sometimes, however, it was more than he wanted to know.

'Helen says Kit has had a difficult time,' his mother had said, confirming the instinct he'd had about the new midwife almost at once. 'A bad break-up. She's fled here, really. I don't know the details. I'm not even sure if Helen does—apparently Kit has kept most of it to herself—but I know she's worried. Be a friend to her, won't you, Gian, until she's settled in?'

This, after he'd already yelled at Kit a couple of hours earlier. Still, one dinner should do it. She seemed attractive, thoughtful, warm. The kind of woman most men would at once want to know better. It shouldn't take her long to make friends in a place like Glenfallon.

'Friday sounds good,' she answered him, her smile polite and cautious, and he made a mental note to include Emma in the invitation.

The two women were around the same age, early to mid-thirties, and were both single. They were just a couple of years younger than Gian himself. The right age, both of them, if he was eager for any involvement at the moment.

But he wasn't. Not yet. The sense of frustration and anger engendered by his divorce was still far too fresh, even after a year and a half, and he didn't feel remotely ready to embark on something new. He told himself this very firmly as he made a phone call at the nurses' station, watching the way the light fell on the back of Kit's head when she focused on her notes once more.

CHAPTER TWO

'I'LL pick you up at seven,' Gian had said, but he was late.

Fifteen minutes late, at last count, and the clock was still ticking.

During this time, Kit rediscovered how nervous it was possible to get when you were about to go out with a group of near strangers, and had a vested interest in earning their good opinion. She smiled a little at her own foolish reflection in the bedroom mirror, and told herself, 'It's dinner. That's all.'

Emma was supposed to be coming, too, but had told Kit at work today that she wouldn't be able to get there until later in the evening. Her stepmother wanted to be taken shopping.

'I probably don't need to say this, but Dr Di Luzio's still getting over his divorce.' She'd added bluntly, 'I wouldn't guarantee that he's in the market for—'

'Neither am I, Emma,' Kit had cut in quickly. 'I'm not in the market for anything. And anyway, he's only doing this because his mother and my aunt are friends. This is about signing off on his responsibility for helping me to settle in, nothing more.'

Understanding this didn't tempt her to treat the evening casually, however. Relief that Gian was late because it gave her time to get her make-up right soon turned into the creeping fear that he'd forgotten all about it—forgotten to invite anyone except Emma, who couldn't come until late, forgotten to make the promised reservation at the restaurant, forgotten even to phone and apologise for forgetting—and wasn't going to show up at all.

His car pulled up to the gate at seven-twenty, and she hurried out to meet him, wishing Aunt Helen hadn't picked today to give the hens a run in the yard. She had to skirt several offerings of fresh fertiliser on the way.

'I'm sorry,' Gian said through the driver's window as she opened the gate. He leaned a bare, brown forearm across the sill. 'I had a delivery and couldn't chase up my mother just now to get your number to phone. Shall I come in and say hello to your aunt?'

'Oh, no, that's nice, but she's at my cousin's.'

Kit stepped through the opened gate and closed it behind her. Seated beside him a minute later, she felt a little breathless, swamped unexpectedly by the potent aura of his dark masculinity. Was this still the effect of their difficult first encounter, earlier in the week?

Whatever it was, she wasn't used to it. His bulk, his colouring, the way he wore his clothes, all of it was unfamiliar and somehow disturbing. James was compact, clean-cut, civilised. He'd been her blueprint for male good looks for a long time. Despite the fact that Gian Di Luzio's frame was covered by another expensive and very urbane Italian suit, minus the jacket, he seemed a lot less tame than he should.

'Didn't have time to put on a jacket or tie,' he said, as they drove, and she wondered if she'd let her eyes linger too long on his body.

The jacket was lying on the pale leather of the car's rear seat, and his shirt-front had a couple of buttons unfastened. The sleeves were rolled, too, as the March evening was warm. He had strong arms, a testament to the work he must do around his mother's farm, and she guessed that his skin would retain its natural tan even after weeks away from sunlight.

'Will you need to put your jacket on at the restaurant?' she asked him, a little short on small talk suddenly. 'Does Glenfallon run to that sort of formality?'

'Kingsford Mill will expect it of the town's obstetrician,' he answered. 'Do you know it?'

'The restaurant? No. I think I remember when it was still a flour mill, when I used to come here for holidays as a child.'

'They did a beautiful conversion on it, and now that the gardens are growing up it looks great. There's a bed and breakfast there as well.' He must have caught the nervous way she smoothed the skirt of her black dress across her thighs, because he added, 'So you're dressed just right.'

The reassurance didn't take away the jittering inside her, and she wondered if he'd noticed just how tense she was. There was an abruptness and a distance to his manner that might be explained by his reaction to her own nerves.

The drive took only ten minutes, and there were several people waiting for them at a table in the bar. The GP who'd assisted in resuscitating Laurel Murchison's baby girl on Monday, Pete Croft, was there with his wife Claire. She dominated the conversation to begin with, talking very fast. Pete looked ill at ease and unhappy.

Also present were Clive Alderson, the anaesthetist, and another GP and his wife, who was a local pharmacist. Finally, there was the couple who owned the Glen Aran winery and leased Federica Di Luzio's land, across the road, for some of their vines.

'Sorry we're late,' Gian told the group. 'Mary Fantauzzi had a healthy boy, Pete, you'll be pleased to hear.'

'At forty-seven. That's great!' he answered.

'She did well, too, but I'm giving her another couple of

days in hospital because there'll be no break for her once she's home with her brood.'

'Yes, I was going to have a word with you about that.'

Gian made introductions and they moved to their reserved table in the restaurant. Emma joined them just as they were about to sit down. Kit was relieved.

'I thought you couldn't get here until much later,' she said quietly to the other midwife.

'I know, but…' Emma flapped her hands. 'Never mind.'

She looked as if she'd dressed in a hurry and hadn't made much of an effort at that. It was the first time Kit had seen her out of uniform. Her mass of dark hair was loose, but not very carefully styled, and her black trousers and cotton top didn't look quite dressy enough with flat shoes.

Something had obviously happened at home. Her colour was high, and she seemed upset and angry, with none of the calm and control she displayed in the unit.

'Are you OK?' Kit whispered, when she found herself seated on Emma's right.

'Thanks for asking… Thanks for *noticing*!' Emma gave a short laugh and bunched her glossy hair with one hand, to let it fall down her back. 'I had a big fight with my stepmother. A *huge* fight,' she amended.

'Oh, not good.'

'No. She says she's moving out. I don't know whether to be glad or sorry…or to take no notice because she won't actually go. She's threatened to before. This time, it seems more serious. She said some awful things!'

'Take a deep breath,' Kit said. 'Don't worry about it tonight. Enjoy yourself.'

'Thanks. I'll try. Certainly don't want to lay it all on you. This has been going on for a while. Sometimes I wish my dad *had* left her the house. But then—Oh, lord, *stop* me, will you?'

'Here are the menus. Decide what you're going to have.'

Emma thanked Kit again, and turned her attention to mulling over the possibilities of soup or salad or seafood. Kit caught Gian's gaze directed at her down the table. He was checking that she was all right. They were a long way apart, and on opposite sides. She smiled at him, to show that she was doing fine, and he smiled back.

Something happened.

Just in the space of that smile.

A recognition of possibilities, and a connection. A reason offered for her earlier jitters in his company. A new dimension to the friction between them a few days ago.

It was silly, and strange, when they'd smiled at each other several times before. Why now? Why should it crystallise into something different now? Was it the soft lighting, perhaps? Or the white wine she had begun to sip?

'I want her to go,' Emma said. 'That's terrible, isn't it?'

'Not necessarily,' Kit answered.

She dragged her gaze away from Gian's, heart thudding, no idea what to think or feel.

'It's five years since Dad died. I felt I had to give her a home. She only has just enough money to live on as it is. She and Dad were only married for two years, before his death. Stupidly, of course, I thought she'd be grateful, even though, to be honest, we never got on very well even when—Oh, Kit, I'm so sorry!'

Emma slumped in her seat.

Gian was looking at Kit again, frowning a little. 'Everything OK?' he mouthed.

'Fine. I'm fine. I'm having the Caesar salad and the seafood linguini,' she said to him, across a gabble of voices.

'So am I,' he said.

Beyond the surface of their words, much more was exchanged.

'Emma, please, talk about it, if you need to, and don't apologise,' Kit said to the other midwife.

There was a string with a magnet attached, and it was pulling her head to look back down the table at Gian. Or that was how it felt. His mouth looked smooth and soft, and there was a light in his eyes, and a depth she could have drowned in.

'Seems like you need to download,' she added, turning quickly back to Emma again.

'Yes, well, the old emotional hard drive has been getting pretty clogged lately.' Emma dabbed at her eyes with her napkin. 'I mean, I'm thirty-three years old, and I can't bring a boyfriend home. When I have a boyfriend. Which hasn't been for...' she looked at her watch '...eight months, three days and twenty-two hours. Not that I'm counting. And he and I had nothing in common anyway.'

'If she really does go, will you feel guilty?' A tiny glance told Kit that Gian was still looking at her, despite contributing very adequately to a lively conversation between the vintner, the vintner's wife and Clive about wine. His face showed the same intrigued, confused and rather awestruck expression she had to fight to keep from appearing on hers.

'Yes. Very guilty. And blessedly free,' Emma said. 'Guilt *may* win, and I'll end up begging her to come back.'

Focus, Kit!

'Doesn't sound like she should count on that!' she said.

'She says she's going to her daughter's, but I know they don't get on too well either. She'll probably land back on my doorstep again in a month.' Emma suddenly sat up straighter. 'Do you know what? I'm not going to take it!'

'That sounds like a decision.'

'I'm going to tell her that I understand how she feels on several of the issues she raised, but I did *not* take anything from her purse, and if she leaves now, with these accusations still hanging in the air, she'd better understand that I'm not taking her back. Do you know, she hasn't *once* acknowledged that I've kept her under my roof and paid numerous bills of hers as a kindness! She's never thanked me for anything. She's always acted as if it was her right. Really, Kit, I'm *so sorry*. I'll stop now.'

'Honestly, it's fine. Wicked stepmother stories are a great ice-breaker, you know.'

She was rewarded by Emma's surprised snort of laughter.

Gian raised his glass and called out, 'What do you think of this, Kit?'

She picked up her own glass and it caught the light, the contents looking mellow and golden. 'Lovely! Very…I know nothing about wine, by the way…fragrant and fresh. I've got a terrible head. I'll only have this one glass, but it's scrummy.'

'There you are, Rick,' Gian drawled. 'Put that on this year's label. Scrummy.'

Why was it so hard to take his eyes off Kit? he wondered. It wasn't the wine. They'd smiled, and something had happened inside him. He'd suddenly felt as if he'd known her forever, and at the same time as if there was a whole world called Kit McConnell that was just waiting for him to explore.

It wasn't at all the way he'd felt about his distant cousin Ciara. He'd fallen in love with Ciara nine years ago, against the backdrop of her native Sicilian soil, when he was twenty-five and she was just nineteen. She'd been darkly beautiful, passionate, illogical, open about her own selfishness, charming most of the time and exhausting the rest. He was in love with a tornado, he had sometimes thought.

He'd waited five years for her, flying to Italy whenever he could and flying Ciara out here. She was too young, he

considered, and he hadn't wanted to force a commitment
from her too soon. He'd thought he was doing everything
necessary to make sure that they were both certain of what
they felt, and yet it had all fallen apart after less than three
years.

Whatever the meaning of these smiles and these clashing
glances, he knew Kit was nothing like his ex-wife.

'Scrummy?' Rick Steele echoed, grinning and sceptical.

Gian returned to the here and now, a much better place
to be.

'It's a technical term,' Kit said. She realised belatedly
aloud, 'Oh, is this one of yours, Rick?'

She reached for the bottle, which Gian was passing solemnly down the table, and took a closer look. '"Glen Aran
Cloverfield Chardonnay"',' she read aloud, and remembered that there was a field on her aunt's farm, bordering
the Di Luzio's property, which was planted with pink and
white clover in some seasons. This gave the wine a personal
connection, and made Kit herself feel as if she was already
halfway to belonging here in Glenfallon.

She read the whole of the wine label at a muttered vol-
ume, raising her eyes at the mention of 'peach and citrus
notes'.

'Sorry, Rick,' she said. 'Gian's right. I'm perfectly happy
with "scrummy".'

Gian laughed again.

'That was a nice night, last night,' he said the following
afternoon, in the sunny yard of the farm.

'I enjoyed it very much,' Kit agreed. The words were as
bland as could be, but she knew the tone gave away too
much. The awareness between them was already thick and
warm and making her dizzy.

'Pete and Claire seem to be having some problems.' He

frowned, and his eyes narrowed. A breeze caught his hair, ruffling it. 'It did get a little tense, towards the end, when they let some of it show. They separated for a while last year, and I'm not sure if the reconciliation will last. Nice if it did.'

'Emma was upset, too, about her stepmother.'

'I think a lot of people know that relationship's not too sweet.'

'But I appreciated the fact that she confided in me. I like Emma.'

'And she's good at her job.' He raised his voice and called, 'Bonnie, sweetheart, can you not yell and jump near the chooks' fence? You'll upset them, and they won't lay.'

He and his little niece had come to collect some eggs, which apparently Bonnie was very excited about. They didn't keep fowls at Federica's. The child quietened down a little at her uncle's words, but not enough, and he went up to her, crouched down to her level to speak more firmly. His shirt stretched across his strong back.

'Hey! Shush, OK, or I won't let you help me,' he said. 'We have to collect eggs *quietly*.'

'O-tay, Untle Zian.' She nodded solemnly, her big, brown eyes fixed on his face.

Kit's eyes were fixed there, too. Or rather, they were fixed on the whole scene. She felt ridiculously jittery and churned up. Had done so ever since Aunt Helen had casually mentioned at lunch that the pair would be coming over later, while Helen herself was out.

Gian had brought a bag of freshly picked Roma tomatoes from Freddie's vegetable garden, and a big bunch of pungent basil as well. The aniseed-like aroma of the leaves still clung to him after he'd deposited them on the kitchen table. It was drowned only by the gamier odour of the farmyard when Kit accompanied him and Bonnie outside.

Bonnie was gorgeous. A mouth full of little white teeth that showed whenever she smiled. Dark ringlets all over her head. At almost two, her hair had never been cut. Darker eyes, just like Freddie's…and like Gian's.

He was dressed like a farmer today, in old denim jeans, which clung with loving emphasis to strong thighs and a tight rear end, and a khaki shirt with rolled sleeves and a frayed collar. Brown, elastic-sided boots and a battered Akubra felt farmer's hat tilted low on his brow completed the picture. His white teeth emphasised his olive skin, and the tiny crow's feet around his eyes made him look as if he was perpetually ready to smile.

'You need a truck, instead of a European car, today,' Kit told him, following her own train of thought. 'And slightly more sun-damaged skin.'

He frowned. 'Oh, I do?'

'That didn't make sense, did it? To make the "farmer in his natural habitat" picture complete and accurate, I mean.'

He laughed, the same way he'd laughed last night. The sound was soft, appreciative, musical, thoughtful. 'Mum has the truck,' he said. Kit loved the way his mouth moved when he spoke.

'Borrow it next time,' she suggested. 'I'd like to see you with your elbow stuck out the open window, and a sheep-dog panting over your shoulder.'

Good grief, was she flirting with him? That was insane! They had to work together. Why was she letting one or two delicious yet dangerous looks and laughs last night make her so bold? Even if there was something to it…a seductive possibility hanging in the air…she didn't want it. She wasn't ready for it. She ought to run a mile!

He muttered something, and it might have been those same words.

I ought to run a mile.

Then he stepped closer.

'Look, this might be a little sudden...' he began.

Bonnie was circling his legs as if they were a tree trunk and she was playing a round-and-round game. He was standing close enough for Kit to see the way his sooty eyelashes feathered so darkly against his skin.

'I—I don't think so,' she murmured, woolly-witted.

'But would you like to go out again?' he finished. 'Just the two of us this time? We didn't get a chance to talk much last night, and I...found that I wanted to.'

I ought to run a mile.

'Yes, that would be—I'd like to, yes,' she answered clumsily, ignoring the fluttery and almost queasy feeling in her stomach.

'Are you free next weekend?'

'No, I think I have some afternoon shifts. I'll have to check my roster.'

'So it would have to be during the week?'

'Or we'd have to wait.'

Unworded between them was the knowledge, suddenly, that neither of them wanted to do that.

Too fast, much too fast. Think first.

Kit ignored the panicking voice of reason inside her head.

Bonnie dragged on Gian's legs, her fists full of faded denim.

'Want to check on it right now?' he suggested softly. 'Could you? Bonnie's very keen to find those eggs, and with my schedule, if we don't arrange it now...'

'I have a copy of the roster in the house.' She knew she sounded as breathless as she felt.

He smiled. 'We'll still be here when you get back.'

Kit headed for the house, surprised that she could walk straight. Aunt Helen was still out, and the place was very quiet. Cool, too, after the March sunshine outside. It still held considerable heat in this part of the country. She needed the coolness, and her mouth was dry.

She poured a glass of water from the tap at the kitchen sink, and sipped it as she went along the silent corridor to her room. Its windows overlooked the yard, and she could see Gian and Bonnie, questing very seriously for eggs. The hens were radical nonconformists, and frequently disdained their designated laying boxes.

Kit's roster was pinned to the small pressed-cork notice-board on the back of her door, and it confirmed what she'd remembered. She had afternoon shifts on Friday, Saturday and Sunday, but Wednesday and Thursday nights were free.

I ought to run a mile.

She just hadn't expected this. Not so soon. Her heart still twisted with the pain and anger of drawn out betrayal every time she thought of James. It wasn't that she still loved him. She didn't think that she did. She couldn't, after all he'd done to kill her feelings. But that didn't mean she was 'over' him, over everything that had happened between them. How could she be, when so much of its legacy still lingered?

And she had given no thought at all to the future, no thought as to what she would do if a man that she liked asked her out.

Ought she, on principle, to turn Gian down? Or accept his invitation but warn him...warn him...*warn* him about all that she couldn't provide, warn him that James had found her crucially inadequate in the end.

It seemed so stupidly premature to be considering all this on the strength of a smile or two, a sense of awareness and heat and an invitation that contained more nuances of meaning than it should.

Outside, she heard him and Bonnie counting. 'One, two,

three, four…' Counting eggs. Counting their chickens before they were hatched.

Is that what I'm doing? she wondered.

Counting chickens. Borrowing trouble. Putting the cart
before the horse. Making assumptions.

He'd only asked her for a meal. If she refused, he'd think
it was personal. And it *was* personal, only it wasn't about
him.

'How about Wednesday or Thursday?' she suggested,
when she stepped out into the sunshine again.

'Wednesday,' he answered decisively. 'Pick you up? I'll
probably be at the farm anyway.'

'Then that makes sense.'

'Sevenish? If it's nice, we could pick up a pizza and go
to a park. Make it a picnic.'

'That sounds lovely.'

Bonnie leaped about once again, singing, 'Eight eggs,
eight eggs, eight eggs!'

Gian carried them carefully in the crown of his crumpled
hat. With the hat off his head, he had 'hat hair'. The thick,
dark waves were a little squashed against his scalp and his
temples. Kit's fingers itched to comb through them, putting
them back in place.

'You found a lot, Bonnie,' she said to the little girl, as
a necessary distraction. 'Are you going to eat one for your
dinner?'

'Yes, and bekfass.'

'Yum! Eggs are good, aren't they? Especially fresh ones.
Would you like some tea or a cool drink, Gian?' she added.

'Not today. Just an egg carton, if you have one. Should
have thought to bring one of our own.'

'I'm sure we have some inside.'

She headed for the kitchen door and he followed her.
Bonnie was still chanting, 'Eight eggs! Eight eggs!'

'Are you sure about the tea?' Kit asked again, over her shoulder. She felt breathless. 'If you're coming in for the carton…'

'I ought to get Bonnie out of your hair. I'm sure you have things to do.'

'Bonnie's fine. We have a box of kids' toys for occasions like this. My aunt has four grandchildren now.'

'You like kids?'

Kit's heart lurched in her chest. 'Yes,' she said lightly. 'Kids are great.'

'Still…' He looked at his watch and frowned. 'Not today.'

Kit rummaged in a cupboard and produced the egg carton. Gian and Bonnie counted the eggs out of his hat, one by one, and then they were ready to leave. The house seemed even quieter after they'd gone.

Kit encountered Gian at work on Wednesday morning. She took over from another midwife at seven, assisting with the labour of one of Gian's private patients, a first-time mother aged thirty-nine.

Jenny Smith's labour had gone slowly but without complications, and things were starting to hot up now. Jenny was finding it harder to manage the pain of the contractions. She tried a hot shower, tried leaning against the bed, and her husband tried pressing a tennis ball against her lower spine. None of it seemed to help any more.

The first Kit knew of Gian's presence was his voice in the doorway.

'Tell me, Jenny,' he teased the patient 'have I got time for a cup of coffee?'

'I want you to examine me and tell me you absolutely *haven't!*' she managed to tease back, though her voice dropped to a whimper at the end of it.

'Good idea,' he said, reaching for a pair of gloves as Kit stepped back from the bedside. 'Let's give everyone some encouragement.'

His assessment was quick and deft.

'Almost there,' he announced, after a moment. 'Baby's still a little high, but you're almost fully dilated, Jenny. A good nine, or even nine and a half centimetres. No wonder you're feeling uncomfortable!' He listened to the heartbeat, and reported, 'Good and strong. I'll skip the coffee, just make a phone call instead.'

'Will you? Oh, *good*!' Mrs Smith said emphatically. Five minutes later, she gasped, 'I think this might be it. Yes, this is it!'

Kit pressed the buzzer and Gian reappeared very quickly. After another check of the baby's position, he told the labouring woman, 'The head's still not very far down, so you've got to do some good, strong pushing, OK?'

'Work with the contractions, Jenny,' Kit added. 'We'll talk you through it. Are you ready?'

'Yes. Yes, it's coming.'

Over an hour of pushing was needed to get the baby's head to crown. Gian had to leave, at one stage, to take a phone call. He disappeared and returned unobtrusively, however, and Kit wasn't even convinced that Jenny knew he had gone. She was getting tired and discouraged again, until Gian told her, 'You're having a blonde, Jenny.'

'A what?'

'A blonde.'

'A *blonde*!' She was half laughing, half crying. 'You can *see*?'

'Yes, crowning beautifully now, and not slipping back, a gorgeous golden blonde.' His eyes met Kit's for a moment.

'I'm having a blonde. Come on, baby girl…'

The concrete reality of the baby's head of hair encouraged the labouring mother hugely. She gave several mighty pushes through the next two contractions, and the head bulged forward, floated steady between contractions and came out with the next push. No cord around the neck. No sign of any problems. Gian rotated the head gently, ninety degrees, and first one shoulder slipped free, then the other.

'She's out,' he said. 'She's here, and she's beautiful. Congratulations!'

The baby cried, and so did Mrs Smith. Her husband Gordon seemed choky and tearful as well. 'She's great. You were amazing, love!'

There were no problems, postpartum. Gian delivered a healthy placenta several minutes later, while Jenny held her naked baby girl in her arms. Little Martha Marie took the breast easily, the suction stimulating the uterus to contract effectively, which reduced the risk of haemorrhage.

A few minutes later, Gian said to Kit, 'I'll see you tonight.'

'Yes… You were good. You were lovely,' she added, a little huskily.

'Don't sound so surprised about it,' he teased, and his grin turned her insides to melted butter.

Kit spent the rest of an uneventful shift wondering what on earth she was doing, feeling this way, when just a few days ago she had felt so far away and so safe from anything like this.

The pizza and picnic plan didn't work out. By the time Kit reached home, just before three-thirty, it was raining. The gutters ran like rivers, the sky was low and dark, and there was no evidence that it would let up any time soon.

'The Glenfallon Bakery?' Gian suggested instead, as they drove into town.

He was casually dressed in dark trousers and a grey shirt, the same colour as the clouds darkening overhead, as the sun dropped out of the sky. Kit wore stretch trousers and a leather jacket, and doubted that she'd be taking the jacket off, since she had short, silky sleeves beneath it. The windscreen wipers on Gian's car clacked back and forth at a rapid rhythm.

'The bakery sounds nice,' she answered him. Casual enough that it wouldn't lend too much importance to the evening. She was shying away from that, nervous about it. 'Is it open this late?'

'Since they expanded to take over the old bank building next door, yes. It's as much a restaurant as a bakery and café now.'

He didn't touch her as they got out of the car. They were both being a little cautious with each other tonight, as if they'd rethought, in a more rational frame of mind, those telling moments over the weekend when they'd both sensed that something was in the air.

I'll ride it out, Kit decided. We'll have a pleasant evening, and he won't ask again. There'll be no need ever to tell him about…

She didn't word the rest of the thought in her mind. It trailed off in a series of uncompleted scenes from her past and from her imagination. Scenes that involved James and Gian, medical specialists, pain and discomfort, arguments, silences and the innocent woman in Canberra who would, by this time, be heavily pregnant with James's child.

CHAPTER THREE

'I WASN'T expecting this,' Gian said, a little later in the evening.

'Dessert? You ordered it.'

'Don't pretend. I'm serious. And you know what I mean.'

Yes, Kit did, and it frightened her.

He touched her hand across the table, his fingers communicating the promise of much more than just this chaste contact as they stroked her skin. She found herself thinking about how it would feel to get closer, to know more about the way he could touch her, and knew that he wanted her to think this way.

She couldn't meet his eyes, and had to look down, which meant she was looking at their hands. This didn't help. She took in the contrasts in skin tone and texture, and felt the heat of awareness flood higher and higher up her arm.

I shouldn't have let it get to this point.

They had kept the conversation light and general for the first part of the evening. He'd talked about the local tourist attractions—which ones he recommended and which ones he didn't. Then he'd talked about what it was like to practise medicine here, when most specialists shunned rural Australia, and hospitals in towns even as substantial and pleasant as Glenfallon had trouble attracting the medical staff they needed.

'Dad's death was a big factor in me coming back, of course,' he'd told Kit.

After this, they'd talked for quite a long while about

family bonds, priorities, goals. He'd touched on his divorce, beginning with his formal separation from his wife, eighteen months ago.

'Yes, I've come out of a serious relationship fairly recently, too,' Kit told him. 'Not a marriage.'

But to her it had always felt like one. She'd made the same 'for better, for worse' commitment to James that she would have made if she'd spoken legally binding vows.

It was only after almost six years that she'd discovered his attitude was very different—that he'd felt himself free to bail out without guilt or apology. She wondered if a real marriage and a divorce would have been easier on her heart and her self-confidence, or if it would have been even worse.

Gian didn't say much about how he felt about his divorce, or about the reasons for it, but Kit remembered what his mother had said—the very first words she'd overheard on the older woman's lips, just last week.

'I can't understand a woman not wanting children,' Federica Di Luzio had said.

The comment clicked into place like a puzzle piece, completing the picture.

Gian had wanted children, and his ex-wife hadn't. That, at heart, was the reason for their split.

'You *do* know what I mean, don't you, Kit?' Gian said. He hadn't touched his dessert, and her hand was still deliciously imprisoned in his. 'The sense that this is worth exploring. Like some enticing, magical pathway, with lots of turns and half-hidden glimpses, to see where it leads.'

'Dr Di Luzio!' said a woman's voice several metres away, before Kit could reply. She saw a young woman in a wheelchair propelling herself towards them with a smile on her face. 'My brother only just told me you were in here tonight.'

'Hello, Megan!' Gian was smiling, too. 'I almost said something to the waiter, but I thought you'd be at home. *Resting*,' he added in a stern tone, and she blushed.

Belatedly, Kit realised that the woman was pregnant. It was difficult to tell where she was up to. Around halfway? She must be one of Gian's patients.

'I rested all afternoon, and then I got bored,' she said. 'I'm feeling fine. Is it really that much more important for me to rest than it is for any other pregnant woman?'

'You think I don't tell other pregnant women to rest?'

'Not as often.'

'Humour me, OK?'

'All right, all right. I must admit, I enjoy getting my feet up. Now, you humour me, and eat your dessert, Doctor!'

'Yes, ma'am!'

'Well, I'll leave you to it.' She smiled at Kit, clearly curious although trying not to let it show, then wheeled herself away, to greet another couple on the far side of the restaurant.

'I'm sorry, I should have introduced you,' Gian said. 'She's—'

'No,' Kit cut in abruptly. 'No, you shouldn't have. I mean, it's OK. Let's not create the wrong impression.'

She snatched her hand free of the delicious web of sensation he'd created on her skin—something she should have done minutes ago.

Gian frowned. 'She's a patient, Kit.'

'I gathered that.'

'She's not always in the wheelchair. She has some mobility and can walk with crutches, but she was in an accident several years ago and sustained some permanent damage. I'm keeping a close eye on her, and we'll schedule a Caesarean. This is her first baby…and mine, with this particular set of circumstances. I thought you might have been interested.'

He sounded stiff and cool, and she felt miserable. Her sense of what was happening here swung wildly by the minute, between the conviction that they needed to talk very soon, bring certain issues out into the open, and the equal certainty that she was overreacting by a country mile and there was nothing to say.

Heavens, this was essentially their first date, and the only promise of a second had been in the touch of his fingers on her hand, in the intuitive connection in the way they looked at each other, and in the words he'd spoken, to which she hadn't yet given a reply.

'I—I'm sorry,' she stammered.

'Yes. So am I,' he said, sitting back. His mouth hardened a little. 'Because something's obviously wrong. What is it?'

'Nothing. Me. Being an idiot. Please, enjoy your dessert.' She was sticking to decaf coffee, herself. 'This is such a nice setting for a restaurant, isn't it?' she gabbled, creating the excuse to look around. 'Hard to believe it used to be a bank.'

'Yes, it's quite cosy, even on a rainy night.'

'I think the rain has stopped.'

He ignored her. 'And we were having a nice time until a few minutes ago.'

'Perhaps I just need some fresh air.'

The remainder of his lemon tart disappeared into Gian's mouth, and he brushed a crumb from his full lower lip with the ball of his thumb, then dropped it onto his tongue. The casually sensual gesture caught Kit's gaze and held it.

'Right,' he said. 'We'll pay and we'll leave, then we'll get to the bottom of this.'

He rose to his feet, his height and sure movement as intimidating as the banked fire in his dark eyes. He wanted her to know that he was angry, that he was taking no non-sense…and that every bit of the awareness between them was still there. On that issue, she didn't need his input. She could feel it all too strongly.

Leaning down, he splayed his fingers on the tabletop and looked into her eyes.

'Going to put on your jacket?'

'Mmm.'

'You're right. It has stopped raining. Let's go for a walk.'

'Yes. All right.'

Kit hugged her jacket around her, feeling that it was more for protection than for warmth. Her skin rose in prickly bumps, but it wasn't because she was cold. Gian straightened slowly, watching her, then turned and went up to the cash desk. He counted out several bright notes, the colour of flames, and waved away the proffered change. He was back in less than a minute.

'Let's go.'

As she stood, he ran the palm of his hand down the leather sleeve of her jacket, stroked his forefinger across her knuckles, then laced his fingers through hers. The warmth of his grip sent sensation all the way up her arm, and when he stepped closer to bend and plant a kiss in her hair, her breathing caught in her throat. She could feel his warmth, smell the subtle aura of soap and maleness that clung to him, sense the gravitational pull of his body on hers.

'Don't look at me like that,' he said on a low growl.

'Like what?'

'As if you're scared, and as if you want me to kiss you at the same time.'

'I—'

'Because I *will* kiss you. Right here. Just to prove that

there's nothing for either of us to be scared of. And I don't want to waste our first kiss on an unappreciative audience of couples and workmates out to dinner. I want our first kiss just to be for us.'

'Please, don't—'

'Kit, I didn't think I was ready for this either. I wasn't looking for it at all, and I certainly wasn't expecting it to have this sense of...' He broke off. 'No, can't find the word. But it seems as if, when it happens, our sense of readiness just doesn't count.'

The streets were still wet. Wet and quiet. Only a few cars splashed past, sending up cold droplets of spray. Kit hugged her arms around herself, keeping Gian at bay. She didn't know if it was by accident or design that he walked next to the kerb, bearing the brunt of the water. She suspected there was nothing accidental involved.

'It'll be nicer by the river,' he said.

The terraced lawns of the nearby municipal park sloped down to the water, and there were some huge and ancient eucalypts by the banks, as well as a playground and bench seats, a cycling path and beds of flowers, all of them well lit.

It was too wet on the benches to sit down. Gian didn't even consider it. Instead, he pushed her defensively folded arms down to her sides and pulled her against his warm body as soon as they reached the little gazebo, where musicians occasionally played.

'Now,' he muttered, very close to her mouth. 'Let's get this whole thing on the table right now.'

His lips met hers a fraction of a second later, brushing, coaxing and tasting. Soft and firm, warm and full, drawing her response as strongly and inevitably as salt created thirst. The sound of protest that constricted her throat was meaningless. She closed her eyes and let the moment sweep her away, let her strength sigh against the support of his thighs and his chest, let her mouth fall open and her tongue begin to explore.

He tasted of coffee and lemon, and he smelled just of himself—a rich, woodsy, leathery smell that spoke of strength and confidence and adult desire. He didn't mind that she knew how much he wanted her. His kiss was intended to show her that she wanted him just as much.

That wasn't in doubt. That wasn't the problem.

Well, it was part of the problem, Kit revised. If she hadn't felt this way, hadn't wanted to kiss him so much, then they could have ended the evening with an average amount of courtesy and respect, because she'd have known there was no potential between them for anything more. This way, with the intuition they shared, and their electric physical response to each other, what she knew she had to do was so much harder.

'Please, don't.' She breathed the words against his mouth, and felt the deep, musical gurgle of his laughter. She groaned and parted her lips further.

'Try just a little bit harder, Kit!' he said.

He cupped his hands around her jaw, his mouth tormenting her with deliberate intent. He nipped at her lower lip, salved the make-believe wound with his tongue, made his mouth dance over hers. When an anguished sound of need escaped from her throat, he laughed again.

'You know what, you're not trying at all!'

'You're not *letting* me try!'

'Letting you doesn't count. I want you to fight, Kit.' Finally, he was serious. He pressed his forehead to hers, laced his fingers together in the small of her back so that his chest was a wall of warmth against her.

'Fight me, if you want this to stop,' he went on. 'It doesn't make sense for you to protest, and push, and put up barriers, when I can feel how much we both want this. When I can feel that there's a spark, a magic, that I haven't felt in a long time, that I haven't ever felt quite the same as this, and that I wasn't sure I'd ever feel again. Not like this, anyway. Not this good.'

'If you're looking for an affair…' She looked searchingly into his face, feeling the way her eyes had narrowed, wondering what he would see. Evidence of all the times she'd cried? She'd noticed lines beginning to appear around her eyes and mouth over the past year.

'I'm not looking for an affair,' he said. 'Why place limits? Not *just* an affair, certainly. It's a starting point.'

'I wish you were,' she blurted. 'I really wish you were!'

The repetition ended on a sob, and she broke away at last, hiding her face in her hands.

Behind her, Gian was silent, until at last he growled, 'This isn't making sense, Kit. You weren't ready for this, I know that. Neither was I. We've both come out of other relationships that have, at some level, failed.'

'Yes, so—'

'Having it happen, unexpectedly, is what's suddenly *made* us ready, it seems. Or that's how I feel, anyway. We can take it very slowly, if you like. And we're free to stop it, either of us, if it isn't working out.'

'I'm stopping it now, in that case.'

'No, you're not. Not until you tell me why.'

She sighed. 'This feels so…back to front.' She looked at him, and saw how intently he was watching her. She spread her hands. 'I have to tell you something. Far too soon. I know it's too soon. I wish there were boxes. ''Too soon'' and ''too late'' and ''just right''. But there aren't boxes, there's just one huge grey area, and we're in it, and I have to tell you.'

'Making me nervous, Kit,' he said lightly.

'I know.' She laughed. Then she bit her lip. 'I'll just say it.'

'Go ahead.'

'I probably…more than probably…can't have children, Gian. That's what broke up my last relationship. Not my idea. His. James. He went through the motions for a long time, after we found out—and finding out was a journey in itself—but in the end he decided I was damaged goods, and he—OK, I'm cutting a long story short here. He moved out.'

She paused, pictured Tammy, sitting happily out in the waiting room at Black Mountain Hospital's pre-natal clinic, while the contents of her thin patient file—fertile women didn't know how lucky they were to have a thin file—blurred before Kit's own vision.

Should I mention that part? she wondered. That James acted like a free agent and started sleeping with Tammy before he even moved out of our house? That she had already conceived, purely by accident, while I was still waiting to hear the bad news on our final IVF cycle? That James is going to be a father in a couple of months?

No.

She'd sob if she talked about all that.

Sobbing would not help.

'What is it, Kit?' Gian was saying. 'Hormonal? Mechanical? There's so much that can be—'

'Don't turn into an obstetrician.' She closed her eyes. 'Not now. Please.'

'I *am* an obstetrician! How can I help—?'

She cut in, 'It's endometriosis.'

'Some women can still—'

'I know about some women, Gian. When we tried, it turned out that I wasn't one of them.'

'What did you—?'

'Stop. Please, stop!' She stepped back, saw the way he was still watching her. 'Do you see why I had to tell you this?'

'Let's just assume I'm very obtuse,' he said softly. 'You *tell* me why.'

'Because it would have been too unfair not to. I know you want children. It was the rock your marriage split on, wasn't it? You did, and your ex-wife didn't. Your mother said something to Aunt Helen, and I overheard.'

'Ah. That was bad luck.'

'It was for the best. Telling you now seems…' she took a breath, gave a laugh with no amusement in it '…*absurdly* too soon, as if I'd been thinking you were going to end the evening, tonight, by saying, "Have my baby." But telling you any later, when I already know about the reason for your divorce, would have seemed as if I was trying to…*reel you in first,* or something. Trick you into—No.' She pressed her hands to her temples. 'No, it's too stupid to finish, that sentence. I'm sure you see my point.'

'I'm working on it,' he growled. 'There were other reasons why my marriage ended, Kit.'

'But the crunch, the thing you couldn't get around, was the issue of children.'

'Yes. Yes, at heart it was.'

'You see? This way, we're both all right. We're safe. It's not *hurtful* to have you back off now, before we really know each other.'

'Isn't it?'

'No. Or much less, anyway. We're still safe, both of us,' she repeated. 'I want you to back off. It's sensible. Rational. Because there's an unbridgeable distance between what you want and what I can provide. It's the ultimate incompatibility. Nothing personal about it. It just is. So we won't see each other any more, and we won't get hurt, and life can go on.'

Gian was silent, and she waited.

'Are you going to have this conversation with all the future men in your life?' he said at last.

'Not all. Only the ones I like.'

'That makes sense.'

'It'll be fun, won't it?' Sarcasm dripped like vinegar in her voice. 'Maybe I should just get a T-shirt printed up, or something, instead.'

'What would it say? No. Don't answer that. The humour's too bitter, Kit.'

'Sometimes, it's a relief. Hardly anyone knows. Maybe turning it into a comedy routine might be easier than having a series of dramatic, confessional talks. I'm not enjoying this!'

Gian could hear the strain in her voice, and see in her body how tightly she was wound. He was so tempted to take her in his arms again and tell her it didn't matter.

But it did matter.

She was right about that.

This wasn't the time for rash assurances, for promises he might not, in the end, be able to keep. It wasn't hard to understand how badly she had been hurt, and he'd seen at first hand, with some of his patients, how a couple's infertility could make cracks widen in all but the strongest relationships.

How in heaven's name could he guarantee, at this early stage, that he wouldn't hurt her again? How could he guarantee that if this intuition between them petered out, it would have nothing to do with what she'd said tonight?

He said finally and very carefully, 'It was brave of you

to talk about it, Kit. I appreciate that. And you're right. We need to step back.'

'Yes. More than that.'

'Step back,' he repeated. 'We still have to work together. We have to maintain a way to deal with each other.'

'As distantly as possible, Gian. It doesn't make any sense to do anything else.'

The rain started again—appropriate, given her bleak words. Gian felt several drops on his hands and face, and saw them beginning to bead the waterproofing on Kit's soft jacket. Without the talk they'd just had, he might have grabbed her hand and they'd have run back to his car, laughing and soon soaked to the skin and not caring a bit.

The rain and the chill wouldn't have mattered. He'd have turned on the car's heating at full blast and held her in his arms and kissed her with all the heat and hunger inside him until they were both warm and dry again. Even a ruined jacket wouldn't have seemed important.

But you couldn't destroy two things in one evening. They'd already destroyed any prospect of a relationship between them. The jacket, however, could be saved.

'We'd better get back to the car,' he said. 'In fact, why don't I leave you at the bus shelter and come back for you when I've picked it up?'

He had parked just a couple of hundred metres further along, outside the restaurant and within sight of the place where he was proposing to leave her.

'Yes, all right,' she agreed. 'It must be getting late. There's hardly anyone about.' Her tone was bright, but it wobbled. She wasn't quite carrying off the 'I'm OK, and I'm not thinking about it any more' thing.

They walked side by side up towards the road, quickening their pace as the rain grew heavier. There was no one else at the bus shelter, no more buses tonight. It was already after ten. Ducking out of the shelter again, Gian began to run, and didn't stop until he reached the car, his wet shirt and trousers plastered uncomfortably to his skin. The sky had opened up, and it was pouring now.

He looked back along the street. Kit made a lonely figure, beneath the shelter's roof, her face very pale and her feathery hair softening the shape of her head. She'd hugged herself again, running her hands up and down her arms as if she was cold to the bones and needed the heat of the friction.

Gian felt a sense of loss that was too sharp, considering how little they knew each other. Infertile couples had to grieve for the death of hopes and possibilities. It must feel a little like the way he felt now.

He hadn't lost someone he loved, but he'd lost the possibility of loving—loving this particular woman, whose scent and smile had bewitched him, who could deal with their professional differences sensibly, who cared enough about family to come and live with a widowed aunt, and who didn't have a good head for wine, or the right words to describe its taste.

The restaurant was closing, he noticed.

Places didn't stay open late on a weeknight in Glenfallon. People had to make their own entertainment. He heard a carload of young men roaring down the street in a hotted-up old Holden. They slowed as they approached the bus shelter, and Gian floored the accelerator pedal of his own vehicle and pulled in beside Kit just as the Holden turned to come back for a second look at her solitary figure.

'I shouldn't have left you here,' he said, feeling as if he'd abandoned her twice in the space of minutes.

She lifted her chin. 'They're pretty harmless, I think. In any case, I know how to use a bunch of keys.'

She held up a fist, and he saw that the slits between her

tightly held fingers each bristled with a key. She gave a faint smile that didn't quite reach her brown eyes.

So she had been nervous, he realised, despite her denials, despite her independent stance. There was nothing he could say. After what they'd agreed tonight, he wasn't the man to offer her any kind of protection. This fact underlined how separate they were.

They didn't talk much during the drive. Kit asked if she could switch on the radio, and they listened uncaringly to an announcer's upbeat patter and half of a current hit. When Gian reached out and pulled her into his arms just as she was about to duck out into the rain to open the gate leading into her aunt's yard, he hadn't planned the moment, it just happened.

She made a sound of surprise and feeble protest as his lips touched hers, but he ignored it, and parted them slightly to make the touch of his mouth soft and sweet and slow. Their kiss didn't last long.

'Just to show that nothing else in the way I feel has changed,' he said. 'Thank you for your company.'

He left her to interpret the words any way she chose, and went to open the gate.

'You can shut it on your way out,' she told him when he came back to the vehicle and drove through. 'The sheep are under a tree, asleep and keeping out of the rain. They won't wander in and bother the dogs at this time of night, or vice versa.'

He wheeled around the muddy yard and pulled in as close as he could to the small porch which led to the kitchen door.

'Um…' she began, and, thanks to her awkwardness, he guessed her intent.

'You're going to ask me in, because you think it's polite,' he said. 'Or because your aunt will expect it.'

'Unfortunately, yes, she will. It's only because she—'

'Because she cares. I know. I have one of those in my life, too. It's not just Italian mothers, then?'

'No, Scottish aunts as well.'

'Tell her my pager went off.'

'Very convenient!'

'Mostly, it's not. Mostly I'm just getting into the shower, or sitting down to a meal. For once, let's give the damned thing a chance to work in our favour. I shouldn't come in, Kit.'

'I know. No sense in…creating expectations.'

'How much does your aunt know?'

'About why James and I split? She doesn't. I don't talk about it to many people. Not fun, dwelling on the details.'

He recognised her indirect plea for him to keep his mouth shut around the hospital, and at home, and it was oddly hurtful to learn that she would think such a warning was necessary. He swallowed and said, 'Hell, do you really think I would, Kit? Do you think I'd breathe a word?'

'James did, at first, to his mates. Until I yelled at him.'

Gian swore.

'Oh, gosh, I think I just heard your pager going off,' she said tightly, and was up the steps and through the kitchen door, her shoes clattering wetly on the cement porch, before he could reply.

His pager hadn't gone off, of course, but he knew why she'd said it.

Aunt Helen met Kit in the middle of the kitchen. The television was on in the other room.

'You didn't ask him—?'

'His pager went off. And I wasn't sure if you'd still be up.'

Aunt Helen looked guilty. 'Well… I waited up, actually.'

'Oh, bad, wicked woman! Just because it was Gian?'

'Well, yes. Freddie obviously thinks he's the greatest thing since sliced bread, and I do remember him being a nice boy.'

'Sliced bread? A nice boy?' Kit laughed helplessly, the wildly swinging emotions of the evening having frayed her completely by this time. 'He'd love to hear that, I'm sure, as a highly regarded obstetrician with about ten letters after his name!'

There must have been something a little metallic in her tone, because it earned her a sharp glance from her aunt. 'Did it not go well, Kit?'

'No, it was lovely, but we agreed… Well, let's just say, please, don't get any ideas. It's not all that long since his divorce, and my—my *break-up*.' She spoke the word with distaste.

'No, of course,' her aunt said quietly. 'You're right. It's far too soon. Freddie's such a romantic, and she's been giving me ideas. I'm sorry, Kit. You know I only want to be able to write to your parents that you're happy here.'

CHAPTER FOUR

'SHE went!' Emma Burns said to Kit on Friday afternoon, the moment Kit entered the unit. The other midwife's brown eyes were very bright, and her hair threatened to escape from the elastic band which she'd failed to wind tightly enough around it.

Kit must have looked as blank as she felt. Emma's face fell, and she hit the heel of her hand against her forehead. 'Yes, why on earth should you know what I'm talking about? I mean Beryl. My stepmother. The removal van woke me up this morning.'

'Emma!' Kit exclaimed, then added cautiously, 'That's…good, isn't it?'

Emma's expression was complicated. 'What's *not* good is that it's my only topic of conversation at the moment.'

'It's not,' Kit said. 'You only feel that way because it's the only topic in your thoughts.' She spoke from experience.

'OK, so it's my obsession? Is that what you're saying? That's worse!'

'Round and round and round. I know. I've been there.'

Emma looked curious.

Kit added quickly, 'Completely different issue, same circular thoughts, dragging you down. You don't need to hear about it. Tell me what happened.'

Kit was several minutes early, and the unit sounded quiet. Glancing at the whiteboard on the wall, she saw that there were only two names on it, as well as a line of notations for each patient, conveying basic background information. In this case, both deliveries looked as if they had good odds of being straightforward.

'Well, she hasn't spoken to me since last Friday,' Emma said, after she'd glanced at the whiteboard as well. 'She does talk to her dog, however.'

'What, and he's thoughtfully passed the information on?'

Emma laughed. 'She talks to the dog in front of me, Kit! This enables her to impart certain news while still conveying the message that she isn't speaking to me, and without laying herself open to unwanted questions.'

'A creative solution.'

'Isn't it? So anyway, there were several comments along the lines of "I mustn't forget to order a taxi, must I, Mr Magoo?" Which she's done before when she really wants me to drive her somewhere. I almost offered. On the other hand, there were a lot of banging and ripping sounds coming from her room.'

'Ripping sounds?'

'Packing tape being pulled off the roll. Maybe I was still supposed to have burst into tears and begged her to stay.'

'That's called passive-aggressive behaviour, Emma, trying to manipulate your emotions to get what she wants. I think you did the right thing to resist it.'

'She's been getting worse. I don't think I would have put up with it if she'd been so difficult from the beginning. It's one of those situation where you're in it, inextricably, before you really understand what's going on.'

'But now she's gone. How do you feel?'

'I think,' Emma began cautiously, 'I *think* I feel better than I've felt in years!'

Kit had no reason to feel the same. Her early shift, yesterday, had been a struggle after too many hours of sleeplessness. She hadn't seen Gian, and it was quite possible she wouldn't see him today either. An obstetrics and gynaecology specialist had many other places to be besides the maternity unit.

Gian had two or three sessions of surgery each week, performing procedures such as scheduled Caesareans, tubal ligations and hysterectomies, fibroid removal, laparoscopy, and dilation and curettage.

Kit knew all about these last two procedures from personal experience. They weren't so bad in themselves, but the reasons for having them weren't fun.

Emma assigned her to the care of both today's patients, to begin with. She was brisk and efficient at the desk, talking through what had happened in the unit earlier today. She said nothing more about what was going on at home, but her cheeks were still very pink, and Kit suddenly wondered, Is she going to come down to earth with a great big crash? No matter how difficult their relationship has been, there's going to be an empty place in her life now.

'I've got paperwork to catch up on,' Emma said. 'And I'll get Julie to help. Mrs Coscarelli has only just come in. PROM at thirty-eight weeks.'

Kit understood the medical shorthand easily. The patient's membrane had ruptured prematurely. It wasn't cause for much concern, so close to her due date.

'No labour yet,' Emma went on. 'Dr Hannaford—she's had shared care, midwives and her GP, who's Hannaford—wants to let things go for a few hours and then start her on a drip if nothing happens. Mrs Lucas is doing well, but it's a first-time baby, and she was only four centimetres dilated when I checked at two-thirty. Supportive husband. They're both using the right techniques to help her manage the pain.'

The light load gave Kit too much time to think. It was the same tangled track of thoughts she'd travelled countless times over the past couple of years.

Am I crazy to put myself through this? Delivering babies and checking on healthy pregnancies, day after day, when I can't have a baby of my own? But I don't want to run away. I don't want to cut children and babies and wonderful births out of my life. That would be just adding another element to what I've lost, wouldn't it?

And in some ways it was easier now, when a pregnancy was quite impossible, than it had been during those long years when she'd held out some hope of a baby of her own, and when every month would bring a new disappointment.

She and James had first begun trying for a baby four years ago. Kit's endometriosis had already been diagnosed a year earlier, just one year into their relationship, thanks to her visit to a specialist. She'd had questions about the pain, heaviness and duration of her menstrual periods. As a nurse-midwife she could immediately call to mind the facts about the disease as soon as she'd heard the diagnosis.

Its causes were not yet well understood. Medical specialists didn't know exactly why some women experienced this painful spread of endometrial tissue beyond the uterus, where it belonged, and into the Fallopian tubes and the pelvic cavity—even further, in rare cases. The results were clear, however—compromised fertility, added pain and menstrual difficulty.

Kit talked to James about the fertility question straight away.

'But we didn't want kids for at least another five years, in any case,' he said.

'Well, *you* didn't.'

'We wanted to play first. Enjoy ourselves.'

'I was thinking a bit sooner. Maybe three years. But now I'm wondering if—'

'Either way, three or five, do we have to think about it now?'

'The disease tends to have a greater impact on fertility the more time goes by,' she'd explained carefully.

'Are you saying you want to try for a baby *now*? You're only twenty-eight.'

'Rather than leave it too late, yes.'

James couldn't be convinced, and they used contraception for another year. Then Kit brought up the subject again, and he agreed to 'see what would happen'. Over the course of another year, nothing did. Kit turned thirty, and didn't like it. A generation ago, she would already have been labelled an 'older first-time mother'. Statistically, from thirty onwards, fertility in the female population was already starting to decline.

She summoned her courage and told James, 'I want to see the specialist again, and start getting some help.'

'You know I hate the idea of that. We've talked about this before. I think we should let nature take its course.'

'But nature isn't going to take its course. Nothing's going to happen.'

'Then we won't have a baby. Life doesn't offer guarantees, Kit.'

She tried to understand, to feel her way into his attitude. But she couldn't. She wanted a baby too much. And she'd seen too many examples of how some relatively simple treatments could bring success. The odds of such success dropped as a woman got older, however.

A few more months went by and she said to him, already emotional and upset, 'I don't understand, James. If you had a broken leg, or asthma, or cancer, would you let nature take its course then?'

'That's different.'

'I don't see how. Human beings have been fighting against nature for thousands of years, and not just in medicine. This *isn't* different. Go and live in a cave and eat raw meat and wild berries, if you feel that way about nature.'

'Maybe I should,' he muttered. 'To get away from *this*.'

From *her*? Was that what he'd really meant?

But then, a few nights later, he'd said to her, in the middle of cooking dinner, 'I've been thinking about what you said. If this is really important to you, I'm willing to try some treatment.'

She'd loved him so much that night, had believed that the battle was won, and that the future was rosy.

But even with treatment, she didn't conceive. She had a D and C, an exploratory laparoscopy, hormone therapy. Finally, they tried IVF. James had grown increasingly terse and withdrawn by this time. Kit kept thinking, It'll be all right again, if I can get pregnant.

The treatment was hard on both of them. James learned the technique for giving her the required hormone injections but it 'gave him the creeps', he said. Kit had terrible mood swings, which both of them had to endure.

One day, he told her, 'When you try to pretend that you're happy, when we both know you're in a total snit... Hell, I think it's worse. I'd *rather* you just went with how you really felt and bit my head off.'

She tried to make a joke of it, coming at him with arms scissoring like a crocodile's snapping mouth. 'OK, here I go. Chomp, chomp, James.' But the humour didn't work. He grabbed his jacket and left the house, and only many weeks later did she realise he must have gone to Tammy's that night.

Meanwhile, she went to the clinic and had her third cycle of IVF, hoping even more desperately for success. She and James badly needed to move on, and into a new phase in their lives. The routine of the procedure and its aftermath was familiar now. The same discomfort. The same influx of new hormones. The same initial elation. Maybe this time...

The elation soon settled into increasing nerves and doubt. She became superstitious, in a way she never normally was.

If I see three babies at the supermarket today, that'll mean good luck. If all my deliveries go well this week, that'll be a good sign.

She didn't let herself think for a moment about baby names, or maternity clothes, or what the weather might be like on her theoretical due date.

But a simple blood test showed that her HCG level hadn't begun to rise as it should have done, and then, as usual, she had started to bleed.

'Look, in a lot of ways, it's probably for the best,' James had said when she told him, too devastated for tears. He didn't meet her eyes for a second, and he held her stiffly, when she'd come to him for comfort and the bitter reassurance of shared grieving. 'There's something I have to tell you, Kit...' He'd sworn harshly. 'This is so hard!'

He'd moved in with Tammy that same day.

Yes, life was easier now. Kit knew exactly where she stood, and although she hadn't seen it this way at the time, James was right on that one point. It would have been very hard if, thanks to the clinical actions of doctors in a lab, she'd been pregnant with his baby when he'd left her for Tammy Cleland. At least, this way, Kit had been able to give herself a clean break...

'Nurse?' said the anxious husband of the patient whose membrane had ruptured prematurely.

Kit turned. She was just on her way to check her other patient after her meal break. Mrs Coscarelli's GP, Dr Paul Hannaford, was due in the unit at any moment. 'Something's happening?' she said.

'Yes, she had one contraction about fifteen minutes ago,

and now she's just had two more, less than three minutes apart. The second one—I mean, well, it was the third one—'

'I know what you mean,' she told Mr Coscarelli.

'It was pretty intense.'

'That's quite normal in this situation. Things might hot up quickly now.'

She went into the room, just behind Mr Coscarelli, and saw that Mrs Coscarelli was in the grip of another contraction, so intense that she was unable to talk until it was over. Kit could actually see the uterus bunching tightly through the patient's gown.

'Why was I hoping something would happen?' she said nervously. 'I don't like this!'

'Let's get you up for another walk around,' Kit suggested. 'That may ease things a little. And we'll listen to the baby as well. I have a feeling things are going to happen fast now.'

She didn't have a moment to draw breath for the rest of the evening. And that was just how she liked it.

Aunt Helen's farm offered plenty of opportunity for the sort of activity that drove out circular thoughts. The two of them spent the following morning drenching sheep, with Helen's son-in-law's help. It was hot, smelly work, but when they'd done their quota of beasts for the day, and Mike had left in his truck to pick up some supplies in town, they were left with a sense of satisfaction and achievement which was worth a lot to both of them.

'Mike and I couldn't have got through this lot without you, Kit,' Helen said breathlessly.

'We're only a quarter of the way through.' Kit took a deep breath, and realised that she reeked of lanolin, chemicals and dust.

'I hope you're looking forward to your days off, and have nothing planned!'

'Nothing but more of this. I actually like it.'

In deference to her added years, Aunt Helen laid claim to the first shower. 'And then I'll get lunch.'

It was one o'clock, and they'd been at it since eight in the morning, with just an occasional break to swig some cold water or an enamel mug of tea.

'No, I can start lunch,' Kit said. 'Just give me some ideas.'

'Toasted sandwiches?'

'Sounds good. About six each, I'd say!'

After washing her hands more thoroughly than a surgeon before an operation, Kit sliced tomatoes and grilled bacon. Her aunt then appeared, clean and damp, to finish the task. The shower was heaven—strong and refreshing—and it felt even better to put on clean clothes and consign the sheep-stained ones to the heavy-duty wash cycle.

Kit heard a car bumping along the rather rutted driveway just as she was putting on her shoes, and discovered, when she reached the kitchen, that it was Freddie Di Luzio and her little granddaughter. They waved to Helen and headed straight for the fowl run.

'Collecting more eggs?' she asked her aunt lightly. They'd brought an egg carton with them this time.

'Yes. It's the craze of the moment, apparently. I've told Freddie they're more than welcome, because we've got a glut. Sandra used to take a lot, but now she and Mike are keeping hens as well, and she doesn't need them.'

Federica declined Aunt Helen's offer of lunch, saying that she and Bonnie had already eaten. Kit and Helen took their pile of toasted bacon, lettuce and tomato sandwiches out to the front veranda, where there was a round wooden table and four canvas-backed chairs, and they ate in a very satisfying silence.

Silence, that was, as far as conversation went. There were plenty of other sounds. The faint drone of a plane flying overhead. The caw of a crow. The whisper of leaves in the breeze.

The peace and beauty of the place seeped into Kit's soul as always. Her body ached pleasantly, and although she'd probably be exhausted after her shift later today, she craved the oblivion of physical fatigue. During the three months between her resignation from the hospital in Canberra and her arrival here, there had often been too many hours when she had nothing to do.

Federica and Bonnie came around the corner of the house, bearing just three eggs in their carton today.

'Are we disappointed?' Helen mouthed to her friend.

'Yes, we are, a little.'

Bonnie soon got over it. She drank a glass of home-made lemon cordial, while the three women had tea. Then, since cordial could be gulped down in half a minute, while tea-drinking took longer, she ran about on the lush green lawn—it needed mowing—chasing butterflies and picking daisies from the garden's border of profusely flowering shrubs.

'What a little cutie she is!' Kit couldn't help saying.

'Remind me of that occasionally, would you?' Freddie said. 'She's also a handful, and exhausting! I'm grateful for all the time Gian puts in.'

Bonnie came up the steps to the veranda, and deposited her fistfuls of flowers proudly.

'Shall I make a daisy chain?' Kit offered.

The little girl nodded. She was content to watch, at first, while Kit split one flower stem and threaded another flower through it, but then she wanted to do it herself. Her fingers didn't yet have the dexterity, and half the flowers were ruined. It didn't matter. There were plenty more. After several minutes, Kit was able to lay a little crown of daisies on Bonnie's head. It looked precious against her dark curls.

'I a p'incess,' Bonnie said. She climbed onto Kit's knee, wanting to put her own crown of mashed stems and petals on Kit's head.

Kit hugged her warm little body impulsively. 'Oh, you *are* a princess!' she agreed.

She realised, suddenly self-conscious, that Federica was watching her, and flushed. She tried to hide her hot cheeks against Bonnie's hair. Seconds later the older woman spoke.

'Speaking of Gian,' she said, too casually, 'you and he got drenched the other night.'

'Yes, he did,' Kit answered. 'But I was all right. He left me at the bus shelter, and came back with the car. We'd been for a walk in the park, by the river. Haven't the council made it nice there now?'

She didn't want to talk about that evening. Aunt Helen had had hopes, and it was obvious that Freddie had, too. She still did. The idea made Kit uncomfortable.

'It was nice of Gian to ask me,' she said deliberately. 'But I'm starting to make friends now, and that will let him off the hook!'

On cue, the phone rang inside the house, and she jumped up to answer it. Probably for Aunt Helen, but if it *was* someone she could legitimately claim as a friend—her cousin Sandra, perhaps—she might avoid any more mention of Gian.

It was Emma.

'Um…' she said, 'I was wondering if you'd like to see a movie this evening. Or something.'

'Emma, sorry. I'm working, remember?'

'Oh, damn, of course!' She sounded a little tense and upset. 'And you're the third person I've tried! Lord, that sounded rude! I didn't make a list with you at the bottom, Kit. I—'

'It's fine. Has something happened?' she asked.

'No. I mean, it's silly… I was so happy she'd gone, but now I feel…'

'Let down?'

'Face to face with my own life. Not pleased with what I'm seeing. Wondering if Beryl was just a convenient excuse. I'm in a rut!'

Kit told Helen five minutes later, 'I'm going to leave early and drop in on Emma on the way to work.'

Being honest with herself, she knew she wasn't sorry to have a good reason for avoiding more time with Federica and Aunt Helen. Gian's name would probably creep into the conversation again. Slyly. With the best intentions in the world.

Steeling herself to see him at work was one thing, but having his mother talking about him, oh, so, casually to her aunt, and in the same sentence as Bonnie, was something else entirely.

Emma met Kit at the door of a little weatherboard cottage in one of Glenfallon's older streets. It was a lovely place, particularly the fine old garden, but it needed some work—an injection of energy and ideas, and a coat of paint.

Some of the rooms were bare or furnished lopsidedly, and Emma explained a couple of times, 'Beryl had a desk here,' or, 'This was her room.'

'Why don't you rearrange the whole house?' Kit suggested. 'Go shopping. Paint. Even if you don't feel ready yet. Do it anyway!'

Emma looked at her. 'I could, couldn't I?'

'You *should*,' Kit corrected. 'This place is yours now. Your life is yours.'

'My life is mine,' Emma repeated, as if she hadn't considered it that way before. Then she grinned. 'My head's starting to spin. You know, I nursed Mum when she got ill. Dad's grief was terrible for a good while after she died, and I didn't want to move out and leave him. I was in Sydney for a couple of years, getting some extra qualifications, but I always intended to come back to Glenfallon.'

'People seem to do that.'

'It's a nice town,' Emma agreed, then went on, 'By the time I did, Dad had married Beryl and I got a flat, but six months later Dad got ill, and Beryl couldn't handle it. So I moved back in. I haven't had much time on my own. There's always been some kind of a change on the horizon. Until now. I felt so empty this morning. But maybe it's just a matter of…'

She trailed off, but the far-away look in her eyes was hopeful rather than brooding. She'd started to plan. A minute later, she asked, 'Would you like an ice cream? I have a six-pack of really sinful ones in the freezer. Double-dipped chocolate.'

'Sounds perfect!'

So they wandered around in Emma's back garden, eating ice cream and talking about paint colours, and whether Emma would have to go all the way to Canberra or Sydney to get some good furniture, or whether the two furniture shops in Glenfallon offered enough choice. Kit was almost late for work.

'Could you go down to A and E, Kit?' asked Julie Wong, who was just about to go off duty. 'They have a woman in there with heavy bleeding. Her husband's with her. They think it's a miscarriage, and apparently they're pretty upset.

The emergency department's busy, while we're quiet, so I'll give you the rest of the hand-over report and you can head down.'

'Sounds good,' Kit answered. This was her first shift in charge of the unit, although she'd acted in this role many times in Canberra.

'Actually, there's nothing much to report,' Julie said, and ran quickly through some notes.

They had one patient in labour, and another who'd delivered twenty minutes ago and would soon be taken through into the postpartum ward with her baby boy. Mary Ellen Leigh was handing this patient's care over to incoming midwife Bronwyn Jackson. Within a few minutes, Kit could make her way down to the accident and emergency department, on the ground floor of the hospital's main building.

Coming through an internal corridor, she glimpsed the crowded waiting room, a busy triage nurse and two clerical staff behind the desk. A couple of men sat there nursing sporting injuries, and several more adults waited in the uncomfortable chairs with bored, resigned expressions on their faces. A baby cried, a toddler sat listlessly on his mother's lap and a pale little girl was led to one of the three paediatric beds.

An ambulance pulled into the bay outside, and Kit heard a woman's voice saying tersely, 'I haven't got time. Deal with it, Gary.'

'Sure, Dr Cassidy,' a male voice replied, sounding angry.

'Threatened miscarriage?' Kit asked another nurse at the department's central desk.

'Um, yes, she's up on the board, and on the computer. I'm not sure which room she's in.'

Kit looked at the whiteboard, found the details and found the patient. She'd been put in the quietest room, at the end of one of the department's three main corridors, which were set out like a capital letter E, and she was lying on her side with her feet elevated. Somewhere in her late thirties, with hair highlighted in dark gold to disguise greying threads, she had a disposable blue pad pressed between her legs, and tears running down her cheeks. Her husband held her hand.

'Can you tell me what happened, Mrs Aspinall?' Kit asked gently.

'Well, I'd been having some very slight bleeding…'

'Can we go back a bit? How many weeks pregnant are you?'

'Ten, from my last period.'

'No problems so far?'

Her husband laughed, but it was bitter rather than amused. 'If you count six cycles of IVF as no problems.'

'Well, no, you're right,' Kit agreed. 'I wouldn't call that no problems.'

She almost wanted to tell them, I've been through it, too. But, of course, the words didn't come. There was a barrier in her throat which felt almost physical when it came to this subject, as if all the necessary words had rusted away. Gian was the only person she'd talked to about it in months, and her heart still dropped into the pit of her stomach when she thought back on that scene between them in the park.

Instead, she took a deep breath and asked, 'But the sixth cycle did bring a confirmed pregnancy?'

'Yes. We've known for six weeks.' Again, it was Chris Aspinall who spoke.

'I phoned Dr Di Luzio as soon as the bleeding started,' Mrs Aspinall came in. 'He's been great so far.' Her tone held reproach, as if Gian had somehow let her down. 'But he said just to wait and see. Plenty of healthy pregnancies have some spotting, apparently. But then this morning it was heavier. And redder. And after lunch I started cramping. There was lots of blood. Thick clots. As soon as the cramping stopped, we came in. We…brought part of it. The blood. And tissue. In a bag. In case it needed to be…examined or something. The flow's eased off now, but…'

'Where's Dr Di Luzio?' Chris Aspinall wanted to know.

'I'm not sure,' Kit said. 'I'll have a look at you now, OK? Let's see if we can confirm what's happening.'

She knew she sounded too wooden and stiff. She put on a pair of latex gloves, feeling the familiar coolness and slip of the cornstarch inside them. The light felt too harsh and bright. Mr and Mrs Aspinall still looked as if they didn't really believe they were here, and that this was actually happening. It was too much like a nightmare.

Kit herself felt that in their position she might rather not have conceived at all.

'If you could lie on your back now, Mrs Aspinall, and bring up your knees. I won't use stirrups, but if you could just let your legs fall apart…'

A sheet covered Mrs Aspinall from the waist down. Slipping her gloved hands beneath it, Kit felt the cervix. It was slightly dilated, and she told Mr and Mrs Aspinall this immediately. They understood that it wasn't good news.

Pressing her other hand firmly on Mrs Aspinall's belly, she was surprised to feel the mass of the uterus. It was larger than she'd expected it to be, like a big orange and quite firm. This time, she wasn't sure what to think or what to say.

As she slid her hands out, she saw a movement in the doorway. It was Gian.

'Problem, Rebecca?' he said. He was dressed in green surgical pants and a V-necked short-sleeved top, his arms bare and ropy with muscle beneath his olive skin. He had a blue disposable mask still flapping around his neck. He must have come straight from emergency surgery, and he hadn't shaved this morning.

His dark eyes met Kit's for a moment, and they narrowed a little. The two of them were both instantly aware of each other—aware of the emotional end to their meal three days ago, aware that this was only the first in an endless series of future encounters. The rawness of it would have to fade eventually, wouldn't it? The awareness would fade. Kit would stop feeling his effect on her senses like a physical blow, and his eye contact like a sharp dart in her chest.

'Seems to be,' the patient managed in answer to Gian. Her voice was husky with threatened tears.

'Kit, did you just do a check?' Gian murmured.

'Yes, and the cervix is dilated to one centimetre. The bleeding has tapered off markedly. The uterus feels like an orange.'

Their eyes met once more, but this time they were thinking about the patient.

Gian asked, 'Can you describe the bleeding for me, Rebecca?'

'Um, yes.' She took a deep breath and went through it all. Again. Kit knew about that—going over the same details time after time, to different staff. Sometimes, she had simply wanted to yell, Can't you just read it in the notes? I've said it twelve times, it doesn't change, and it doesn't get easier with practice!

But she knew there were reasons for the repetition. Sometimes a patient would remember something significant, or express something in a new way, which shed a different light on what was happening. And the patient's own words fleshed out the dry facts contained in the notes.

'I'm going to send you for an ultrasound, Rebecca,' Gian said. 'Just to get a fuller picture of what's happening. Kit, if you could get a catheter in, and fill the bladder? I want a really good picture on this, and I'd rather not wait. I'm going to be back in surgery soon. I'll order the scan now.'

He left the room, and Chris said, 'Can you explain? I'm not sure what's happening. What's this for? Why a catheter?'

'Because it's quicker,' Kit said. 'I think Dr Di Luzio wants to look at the ultrasound himself, before he goes back into surgery.'

She got out a catheter kit and inserted the cannula without difficulty, then put in a litre of saline. The hospital's imaging department wasn't quite ready for Mrs Aspinall yet. Kit phoned up to the maternity unit to check that things were still quiet, then paged an orderly to wheel the bed.

She knew that the Aspinalls expected this to be simply a routine confirmation of what they already knew. She also guessed that if Mrs Aspinall hadn't been one of Gian's IVF patients he might have told her much more casually, 'Go home and wait. You may still be pregnant. We'll do a scan on Monday.'

With this couple, he obviously felt that they'd spent enough time on tenterhooks. And if there was a viable pregnancy still in existence, he'd want to do everything in his power to keep it that way.

The orderly arrived, and Kit told the couple, 'I'm not sure if Imaging is ready for us yet, but we may as well wait there as here.' She was paged back to her own unit just as Mr and Mrs Aspinall went in for the scan.

'Have we got customers?' she asked, when she'd greeted Bronwyn at the desk.

'Yes, two within five minutes of each other, and my primie is ready to pop. One of the new arrivals is definitely in established labour. I think you'll end up sending the second lass home. She's not due for two weeks. I've put her on a monitor and she's having contractions, but they're pretty mild and not regular.'

'Wishful thinking?'

'I think so. This is her second, and the first one was big. She's hoping for something earlier and therefore smaller this time. By the way, how did you do downstairs?'

'I hope to find out, eventually. You paged me too soon!'

'Sorry, but your new patients would probably disagree.'

Kit was on the phone to one patient's GP with a progress report when Gian arrived, at around six. Again, he must have just emerged from surgery, and he looked tired. 'I thought you might want to know about Rebecca Aspinall,' he said, leaning over the high desk front.

'Yes, very much.'

'It *was* a miscarriage.'

'Oh, no! When I felt that englarged uterus, I hoped—'

'A miscarriage of one twin. The second twin is doing fine.' He grinned. 'There was a strong heartbeat, and visible movement on the scan. Kid was doing somersaults. We had two very happy parents.'

'Oh, I bet!' She felt the prick of tears, and hoped he wouldn't see them.

'It was great. I've suggested several days' bed rest, just in case. They've been through the mill, trying to conceive. When a miracle like that happens, I feel like I've won an Olympic medal.'

Kit couldn't speak, could only nod. Would have cried if she'd tried to open her mouth and use words. She could tell that Gian knew it.

'Anyway,' he said lightly, 'good news has a ripple effect, don't you think?'

He turned, pulling off the mask he'd once again forgotten about, and she finally found her voice.

'Thanks, Gian.'

He turned back, leaned over the desk again. Bronwyn was coming out of her patient's room. 'You're off at eleven tonight, aren't you?' he asked quietly.

'Give or take a few minutes.'

'Is that too late for coffee?'

'I was drenching sheep all morning.'

'I'll take that as a "yes, it's too late".'

'It's more of a "no, it's not a good idea", Gian,' she answered him helplessly. 'The other night, didn't we…?'

'Yes, we did. But it felt…unnecessarily bleak, don't you think? Unfinished, too. I'd like to tie off some ends.'

The phrase alarmed her. She imagined questions she didn't want to answer, and platitudes she didn't want to hear. He was only attempting to be kind. And if he began to talk of miracles, she might empty the contents of her cup over his head.

'There are always loose ends in this life, Gian,' she said. 'Life's…untidy. If we face each other, and shake hands, agree that we're going to be great friends and that it feels fine, we'll be pretending. I'd hate that. I'd rather have the honesty.'

'And the mess?'

'And the mess,' she agreed.

He nodded slowly, and she realised he wasn't going to argue. With an utter absence of logic, she found out how strongly she'd been hoping that he would.

CHAPTER FIVE

As soon as he had a chance to think about it, Gian realised he didn't buy Kit's reasoning on the issue of how to handle their inevitable future dealings with each other.

Sorry, but he just didn't.

He didn't go out to the farm that night, after finishing work, but took the short drive to his unit near the hospital instead. Although he knew he needed solitude, the place seemed too cold and empty. He took a shower, put on navy Chinese-style pyjama pants and a plain T-shirt, then wandered into his efficient little kitchen, hungry.

The meagre contents of his fridge didn't excite him. Toast and a can of soup would have to do. He ate the toast out of one hand, and the soup out of a mug in the other, pacing between a TV show he wasn't interested in and an electric kettle that wouldn't boil. Some vital component inside it had apparently died. He boiled water for his decaf plunger coffee in a saucepan on the stove instead, irritated more than he should have been by the minor technical setback.

Thought about Kit, and what she'd said.

Honesty, and mess. No pretence of friendship. No coffee together, please, because talking wouldn't help.

In his experience, women usually wanted to talk. A lot.

Kit didn't, and he wondered why. He got the sense that she was running away from more than just the awareness and intuition between them, but perhaps that was only ego on his part. He knew his ego was healthy, as a successful man's ego should be. It made him impatient, slow to accept defeat, stubborn about looking for possibilities and answers.

Equally, however, he didn't want to push. Not yet. He'd wait a while.

'I've got Janet McDowell on the phone, wanting to know if you can squeeze her daughter in this afternoon,' Gian's receptionist, Barb Throssell, told him. She spoke in an undertone, with her hand over the receiver.

He saw Megan Ciancio, with her walking frame propped in front of her, and realised that hers was the next file in the pile that awaited him. There were two more patients waiting as well. Fitting Tracie McDowell in without making himself very late would be a challenge. And he felt irritable. Not up to challenges today. He'd felt this way too often lately.

Janet McDowell had always been pushy, an eager manager of other people's time but perhaps, with seven children, she had to be.

'Any idea why the problem's so urgent?' he asked Barb.

'Severe abdominal pain. Tracie's in tears, I think. Janet seems fairly insistent.'

'Hmm.'

'Panicking, almost.'

Gian suppressed a sigh. 'If she can be here in fifteen minutes. Otherwise, send her to the hospital A and E.'

Seconds later, he regretted the concession. Abdominal pain? It probably wasn't even his area, although Tracie had had some serious menstrual problems over the past couple of years, as well as surgery for a benign ovarian tumour. She had been a stoical patient, he remembered. If she was in tears, perhaps her mother's instincts were right.

'Always listen to the mothers,' he muttered. It was a

piece of time-honoured general practice wisdom that had proved itself in most doctors' lives.

Megan Ciancio made her slow way into his office. Her pregnancy was providing added challenges in her daily life, but from an obstetric point of view, all was well so far. Gian had some test results for her today, and all the news was good.

'The baby's fine,' he said. 'The ultrasound pictures showed healthy, normal development. No problems with size, nice placenta. And your alpha-feta protein screen was normal.' He flipped a page. 'I guess you already knew that. Normal blood sugar at this stage, though we'll test you again for any signs of gestational diabetes later in the pregnancy.'

'Ugh, more of that glucose drink, I suppose.'

'The colder it is, the better it tastes, supposedly.'

'I don't suppose you've even tried it, right?'

He gave a guilty smile. 'Well, no. Do you think I should, in the interests of knowing what my patients suffer?'

'I'll let you off. It's not that bad, really. But yesterday…I was so nervous, having the ultrasound. The technician thought it all looked fine, but I wasn't ready to believe her until I'd heard the same thing from you.'

'Relax!'

'Should I take lessons from you?'

'You're right. I'm being super-cautious with this, too.'

His next two patients were quick and easy to deal with—a six-week postpartum check-up and a routine pre-operative consult with an older woman who was scheduled for a hysterectomy. Gian had just ushered her out when Janet McDowell and her daughter arrived—*not* within the prescribed fifteen minutes, he noted—and he only needed one look at the way seventeen-year-old Tracie was walking, clutching her mother's arm, to understand what the problem was.

It seemed equally apparent, however, that neither the patient nor her mother had the slightest idea.

'She's in a terrible state, Dr Di Luzio. The pain is coming and going. It isn't the tumour grown back? Or that perithingy I've read about?'

'Peritonitis? I doubt it,' he answered grimly.

'Her stomach feels *hard*.'

He didn't waste time ruling out the less likely options. He went with what his instincts told him. 'Tracie, can you lie down on the table? I want to do an internal exam.'

And he didn't want to look like a fool if, by some faint chance, he was wrong. It seemed incredible that neither of the women realised the truth, but it wouldn't be the first time. One touch of the flat of his hand on her hardened abdomen, where the muscles were bunching as she groaned, one practised assessment of the state of her cervix, and he was sure beyond doubt.

Tracie was pregnant, and in labour, and close to full dilation—and there was a fair bit of denial going on in the McDowell family.

He didn't say anything. Not yet. Got out his portable Doppler machine and positioned the receiver right where he thought the baby's heart should be. Tracie was generously built—'big-boned for her height', Janet always phrased it, as well as calling it 'a puppy fat problem'. The pregnancy was therefore well concealed, but no-one could hide the strong, rapid beat of a full-term baby's heart. They all heard it as soon as he switched on the machine.

'Oh, my sainted aunt!' Janet shrieked. The youngest of her own children was only around three, and she'd heard this sound before, not so long ago. 'That's a *baby*! Tracie, how could you *do* this? Telling me it had to be appendicitis!'

'But Mum, I—' The teenager had gone white. 'I'm not pregnant. I'd have known. You're supposed to feel sick, and stick out like a basketball. Lauren Muncie did. I couldn't be. It was only… Jase and I haven't even exactly…'

'Tell me the truth, Tracie. *What* did you and Jason do?'

Gian tuned out the mother-daughter interrogation and reached for the phone. He had the maternity unit at Glenfallon Hospital on his speed dial, available at the touch of a button, and the touch of a button brought him Kit's voice, cool and fresh and professional and familiar.

He had hoped it would be someone else. Three weeks since their decision to step back from what had started between them, and he still couldn't hear her, or see her, or even hear someone else speak her name without a painful twist of frustration and regret and awareness of missed opportunities deep in his gut.

'Sending you a surprise package,' he told her. 'And I'll be following shortly, because I don't think there's a lot of time, and I want to make sure things are OK with this one.'

'A surprise package?'

'For all concerned.'

'Oh, OK, I get it. The stork's bringing it?'

'Something like that. So be on the look out for some friction, and a lot of shock.'

He glanced at his patient and her mother, but they weren't listening.

'I didn't know that was all it took,' Tracie was saying. 'Jase said it was OK. Safe. I can't be having a *baby*!' she wailed. 'I can't be!'

This is going to be hard for Kit.

Gian knew it. He'd seen it before with patients for whom

getting pregnant was an interminable campaign. He tried to schedule his appointments so that infertility patients didn't have to sit in the same room as radiant pregnant newly-weds, or sullen, I-don't-want-this-to-be-happening pregnant teens.

Kit handled it daily, without letting her turmoil show, and he wondered if it was a testament to her strength, her stubbornness or some other quality inside her that no one ever would have guessed how much it must sometimes hurt.

He got to the delivery suite ten minutes after Tracie and her mother, and not one minute too soon. She was already starting to push, fighting against Kit's attempts to calm her. 'I don't know what to do! Unhh!'

'You're doing fine. Just right.'

'No, I'm scared. It feels as if I'm going to—Unhh!'

'Yes, that's great, Tracie.'

'Oh-oh, what's *that*? Oh, it feels—Is this the *baby*?'

'Yes, the head is crowning, Tracie. That means we can see it. And the doctor's here.'

'This is just insane!' Janet was muttering in the background. 'I've got dinner to cook. Alan's not home until six. Kim's looking after Nicole and goodness knows what the boys are up to! How can she not have known? How could *I* not have known?'

'*Mu-um!*'

Kit took Tracie's hand, while Janet supported her shoulders. Tracie's face was red with effort, but the effort was paying off. Gian took possession of a wet, round little head, and the rest of the baby's body rotated and slipped free on its own. It was small, only around two and a half kilos, or just over five pounds on the old scale, but perfectly formed.

Within minutes, the cord was clamped and cut, the placenta was delivered intact, the little girl was cradled in her young mother's arms and the noise and activity and disbelief settled into an oddly precious interlude of peace.

'She's amazing!' Tracie's voice was awed, soft and rough with new emotion.

'She's perfect,' Kit said.

Janet still seemed stupefied. 'I guess another baby's not going to make a lot of difference round our place. Nicky'll treat her like a little sister.'

'I don't know what to do, Mum.'

'*I* do, love, with bells on. I'm not doing it for you, but I'll teach you. I'll help. It'll be all right.'

'It's like she just dropped into my lap.' Emotional sobs broke through in Tracie's voice, like summer rain clattering on a roof, and she was laughing at the same time. 'I thought having a baby was meant to be hard!'

Kit had her back turned. She'd tidied some equipment and was scribbling notes. Gian watched her, could see just by the set of her shoulders that she was struggling with her emotions. A baby had 'just dropped' into this patient's arms, while she'd wanted one so badly for so long, with no success.

He wanted to hit her with a barrage of the questions she hadn't let him ask three weeks ago. How long have you been putting yourself through this? Wouldn't it be easier if you took some time out, and retrained? Aren't you hurting yourself in a way you don't need to? Hurting yourself more than your ex-lover did, or than I could, if we tested what we feel and it failed? Why do you do it?

She pivoted, lifted her face and caught him. Flushed. Obviously knew exactly the direction his thoughts had travelled in.

'Don't,' she said. 'I'm OK. This isn't new after all.'

'No, but doesn't it damage you a little more every time?' he muttered.

'It's not your problem, Gian. This is why I don't tell people. Why I *can't* tell people. I *refuse* to make it into anyone else's problem!'

Her eyes burned, and he felt as if the genuine care he'd tried to express had curdled and turned ugly, clumsy. It wasn't what Kit wanted. All she wanted was distance. His distance. He guessed that if she'd seen any other way to put distance between them, she would have used it. If she'd been able to deny the attraction, she would have done so.

She felt it strongly, then. As strongly as he did.

It all seemed like such a waste.

'And we're invited to afternoon tea at Freddie's, Kit,' Aunt Helen said as they swept the shearing shed. 'We'll have earned it by then!'

It was a Wednesday in late April, the last of four days off in a row for Kit. She'd successfully kept busy on all of them. For the first two days, Emma had been off work, too, and they'd painted part of the outside of Emma's house in an attractive palette of colors—rich cream walls, with a mix of dark, slaty blue and a warm peach for the elaborate wooden trim.

It was a satisfying transformation, from peeling pale mint green to the fresh, pretty colours, and the shared work began to form the foundation of a friendship that Kit hoped would last.

Emma had been busy on her own for several weeks before this, and the exterior of the house was now almost finished. She'd been working on the inside of the house as well, painting rooms, ripping up carpets, revarnishing floors and buying new furniture. She had created some new garden beds running parallel to the front path, too, and had planted them with spring bulbs.

'I'm proud of myself,' she had said to Kit yesterday,

surveying her work as they sat on the veranda, with the autumn sun on their bare legs. They'd been eating pizza for lunch, straight from the box.

'You should be,' Kit had told her, through a mouthful of anchovies, olives and stretchy cheese. She swallowed. 'You've worked like a dynamo, and it looks great.'

The next day, Emma had been back at work, so Kit turned to the work of the farm, and helped her aunt with the sheep. It was good to go to bed exhausted. That way, she slept.

The invitation to the Di Luzio farm should have come as good news. As Aunt Kit had said, by this afternoon they would have earned the break. But Kit had mixed feelings. Would Gian be there? Probably not. It was a weekday afternoon.

Obstetricians kept odd hours, however. She couldn't count on his absence, since she knew how much he tried to help his mother out with Bonnie.

She had been silent for too long. Aunt Helen prompted, 'You'll come, won't you? Freddie definitely included you. You've nothing else planned?'

'No, it'll be lovely. I like Freddie.'

'She was so disappointed when Gian and Ciara divorced.'

Kit blinked at the sudden change of subject. 'Well, I'm sure,' she murmured.

'She was thrilled when he married an Italian girl—she was some kind of distant cousin, from Gian's father's side of the family—and Freddie bent over backwards to be a good mother-in-law.'

'I get the impression that when it comes to bending, Freddie has a pretty strong and supple spine, too!'

'Oh, exactly. She told me she's wondered how much of it was her own fault. If she was trying too hard.'

'I can't imagine that had anything to do with it,' Kit answered. 'When a marriage breaks up, I think it's usually just about the two people concerned.' She added quickly, 'What time are we invited for?'

'Around four.'

They stopped work at three-thirty, needing, as usual, to shower and change. Freddie already had the kettle on and scones just out of the oven when they arrived. The Di Luzio farm was gorgeous, and quite different in its atmosphere from Aunt Helen's, although they were only two kilometres apart.

Firstly, there were the Glen Aran Winery's vines, marching in parallel rows away from the long, straight dirt road leading up to the farmhouse. The grapes had been harvested now, and the leaves were beginning to turn and fall, but at the end of each row there was a rose bush, and most of these were still blooming with untidy pink flowers.

The farmhouse itself consisted of a tiny original wattle and daub cottage, now used as a storeroom and attached by a walkway, half-drowned in wisteria, to a brick house which had been rendered and painted a terracotta pinky-brown, so that it had a definite Mediterranean feel.

There were nasturtiums and geraniums planted in an array of old bathtubs and washing-machine drums and olive-oil cans and wheelbarrows, and in a north-facing sun trap behind the house, sheltered by a high, vine-covered wire fence, there was the vegetable garden, clearly Federica Di Luzio's pride and joy.

Kit glimpsed the basil and tomatoes that Gian had brought over several weeks ago, as well as lettuces and yellow squash, pumpkins and raspberry bushes, spinach and onions, thick asparagus fronds and spiky artichoke bushes. There was probably more, only she didn't have time to see.

Freddie had used the whistling kettle and the smell of the scones to lure them inside.

The kitchen was as bright and welcoming as the farmhouse's exterior had been. As well as the scones, a wide pan of freshly made lasagne sat on top of the stove, ready to go in the oven in time for the evening meal. A big, old-fashioned wooden dresser held shelves of jarred tomatoes, dried herbs and braided garlic bulbs, as well as two wide Italian ceramic bowls filled with citrus fruit.

Bonnie sat at the kitchen table, drawing with crayons and pencils and felt-tipped pens. She had a pile of scrap paper from her Uncle Gian's office, and she was scribbling energetically on each one before consigning it to the pile of completed efforts, changing colours and beginning a new one.

'I'm not sure that it's art,' Freddie commented, as she made the tea. 'More like a factory assembly line. She produces thirty at a time. I don't know what we'll do when Gian's old letterheads run out.'

Kit sat down next to Bonnie, slid a sheet of paper towards herself and picked up a pencil. She drew a fairy princess, complete with crown, wand and wings, and wearing a petal-shaped gown. It was an amateurish effort, but Bonnie seemed enchanted all the same.

'Would you like to colour it in?' Kit suggested.

Bonnie nodded and smiled, and went scribble, scribble, scribble on the fairy princess with a pink felt-tip pen. 'Nuvver one?' she said. 'Pease?'

After such a lovely 'please', Kit could only oblige, and now there were two people working the factory assembly line. She drew fairy princesses, and Bonnie scribbled on them, and Aunt Helen predicted, 'You won't be allowed to go home, Kit, or have your tea.'

'She will be, if I put enough strawberry jam and whipped cream on Bonnie's *sconi*.'

'*Sconi*?' Kit queried. It sounded like an Italian word, the way Freddie gave a lilt to it and lingered on the 'n', but she didn't think it was.

Freddie laughed.

'It was the only Australian thing my mother ever learned to cook,' she said. 'My parents came out here from Sicily after the war, when I was five. Mama's English was never very good, and she called them *sconi*. "*Staio facendo sconi*," she'd say. "I'm making scones." It sounded Italian, and plural, and a little bit like *biscotti*, and was easier for her to say than "scones". I've called them that all my life, and I forget it isn't a real word.'

'It's lovely,' Kit said. 'I'll have two *sconi*, please.'

'Have three.'

'And I'll probably call them *sconi* forever now.'

'Definitely every time you come to our place, anyway.'

The answer implied that Kit would be coming often. She wanted to push the idea away, only that would be rude, and anyway there wasn't the opportunity, because she'd just heard the sound of a car pulling up outside, the squeak of its boot opening and footsteps approaching, and seconds later the kitchen door swung open and there was Gian, with his hands full of plastic shopping bags.

'Oh,' he said. 'Hi.' He smiled, as if mainly because it was expected in this situation, then focused on what was spread on the table, as if seeking a safe subject. 'Mum, you've made *sconi*.'

'Untle Zian! Untle Zian!' Bonnie said, bouncing on her chair.

'Sit down and have some.'

He shook his head, slid a glance quickly past Kit and said, 'I only came to drop off the shopping. And tonight's the night you want me to babysit, right? I'm not on call. Seven, was it?'

'Yes, but come early and eat first.' Freddie gestured at the lasagne on the stove. 'A proper meal. Kit and Helen, will you stay?'

Aunt Helen shook her head. 'We've got Sandra and Mike and the kids coming over.' Kit was relieved that she'd answered for both of them.

'And I can't,' Gian answered his mother. 'I'm sorry. I've got work to do at the office.'

'It could wait,' his mother suggested hopefully.

He smiled again. 'No.'

'He does what he wants,' Freddie said to Helen and Kit and the room in general, raising her hands. She added, 'Which is just as it should be.'

'Could I help unpack, Gian?' Kit offered, out of politeness and, if she was honest, a desire to speed his departure.

His presence seemed to fill the room, commanding the attention not only of Freddie and Aunt Helen, but of the little princess with jam and cream on her mouth. She was holding out her arms to him.

'There's only a few more bags,' he said to Kit, then picked Bonnie up out of her chair and got a sticky kiss which left a dab of cream on his cheek. He felt it and rubbed it off with the back of his hand.

Kit was conscious of every movement he made, didn't know whether to look at him as the others were—Bonnie was also pulling his ears—or to try and hide her face by staring down into her tea. Both responses seemed to give away far too much. She had no idea how to go about behaving as if she didn't feel this way. It was…painful.

To her relief, he put Bonnie back in her chair and disappeared out the door, to return a minute later with the rest of the bags, which he put down on the bench beside the double sink.

'That lasagne does look good,' he said.

'Six, then?' Freddie suggested, recognising his capitulation.

'No, more like six forty-five. Can't get here any earlier. Bonnie can watch me eat after you've gone, Mum. Bye, Kit, Helen.'

Outside, the boot banged shut, then the car door. There was the rev of an engine and a spit of gravel, and he had gone.

Kit felt stupidly, *ridiculously* flat. Just that one taste of his presence and she was starving for more. She had to fight to stop it from showing. While Freddie complained to Helen that Gian worked too hard, Kit gulped the rest of her tea, picked up her last mouthful of scone and asked, 'Could Bonnie show me the garden? Would she go with me?'

'Want to show Kit the veggies, love?' Freddie asked her little granddaughter.

Bonnie nodded and climbed off her chair. ''Matoes. Puntins. 'Kini.'

'That's right, sweetheart. Tomatoes, pumpkins and zucchini. Show Kit all of those. Pick anything you like, Kit. We have too many yellow zucchinis, and the silver beet is going to seed. Masses of tomatoes. The basil is rampant this year. Take some, and make pesto. Gian puts it in Thai curry, too.'

'It all sounds wonderful.'

It took fifteen minutes of pottering around the vegetable garden with Bonnie before Kit could put Gian out of her mind, and when they wandered back to the house and found Freddie and Aunt Helen clearing up the afternoon tea things, she strongly suspected that she had been their chief topic of conversation, and that her name had come up in the same sentence as Gian's more than once.

She wasn't sorry when they left at five-fifteen. She hated the feeling that she was under a microscope, no matter how loving the scrutiny.

Feeling a little remorseful about his lightning visit and abrupt departure, Gian arrived back at the farm at twenty past six, in time to sit and eat his mother's delectable lasagne, along with a salad of fresh greens from the garden, while Bonnie and her grandmother were still finishing theirs.

'Office work caught up?' Mum asked.

'Just about.'

He waited for her to reiterate that it could have waited. That he could have stayed earlier, instead of making the double journey between here and town, but she didn't. She was pretty good, most of the time. Meddled in his life far less than she would probably have liked to do, and never tried to tell him his business when it really counted.

Urging a second helping of lasagne upon him was one thing, and acceptable, but she had sense enough never to touch on what was painfully important. She listened, on the rare occasions when he felt like talking about difficult patients, hospital politics or his divorce, but she never told him what he should or shouldn't do about any of it. He valued her wisdom in that area.

He also appreciated that at times she was quite subtle...

'Kit's lovely,' she suddenly said, when he was halfway through that second helping.

He swallowed. 'Yes. I think we agreed on that several weeks ago, didn't we?'

'Well, but she hasn't disappointed on further acquaintance. Some people do.'

'True.'

'Gian?'

And at other times she wasn't subtle at all.

This was one of those times. He could tell by her face.

'Yes, Mum?'

'You're interested, aren't you? In Kit.'

He controlled a sigh. 'Remember when Ciara ran off to that friend of hers in Sydney, and then phoned you three days later in tears, telling you to send me up there straight away to come and get her?'

'Of course! As if I could forget that!'

'And remember how you didn't ask me one thing about what she said when I got there, or what I said in reply, or what had gone wrong in the first place?'

'I thought you'd tell me if there was anything you wanted me to know.'

'Exactly! Same rule applies now. I'd tell you if there was anything I wanted you to know. OK?'

'OK.'

'Is it? Good. Then there's nothing left to say.'

He ate the rest of his meal in silence, deliberately not looking up to see if she was still watching him.

CHAPTER SIX

'LOOK, I wanted to let you know,' James said on the phone. It was almost four weeks after Kit's visit with her aunt to the Di Luzios' farm.

'Well, thanks, yes.' Kit's mouth felt numb and her legs were shaking. She had known that the baby was due now, but she hadn't expected James to call her himself, with news of the birth.

'Because I knew you'd be bound to hear from someone, and I thought... Yeah. That it would be better coming from me,' he went on.

'Yes,' she answered, hardly knowing what she was saying.

'She had a beautiful baby boy. We're calling him Luke and, of course, we're jazzed about it. I—You know, Kit, looking back, I'm surprised we lasted as long as we did, you and I.'

'Are you?'

'It was nothing to do with the baby thing. With your endometriosis, I mean. Your infertility.'

I get the point, James.

'And the thing is...' he went on.

He's just going to go on and on until I say something, she realised. *Until I let him off the hook and tell him it's OK, he's done the right thing. And every word he says gets worse, so I have to say something. Just to stop him. Before I scream.*

'Of course, James,' she finally got out, in a voice so tight

95

and hard that it burned her throat. 'Of course. Congratulations.'

'Yeah, thanks. I knew you'd...' He stopped and tried again. 'You're such a great person, Kit. Really. Seriously. I wish you'd learn to believe that.'

She wanted so badly to say something obscene, to let fly with a torrent of bitterness, but had just enough sense left to understand that anything she said would haunt her forever, long after James himself had put it down to the 'hell hath no fury like a woman scorned' syndrome and shrugged it off.

Just a tiny bit more control, and she could at least save herself that regret.

'Thanks for letting me know,' she said. 'Look, James, I have to meet some friends.'

'Of course.' She could hear the relief in his voice. 'Sure. Sure. Just wanted to let you know.'

'Thanks. I'm glad you did.' And she was, because now that particular, painful hurdle was behind her and was therefore one less thing she had to dread. 'I really have to go. Bye, James. And I hope it all goes well. With the baby. And everything.'

She put down the phone and went out into the yard, where it was as sunny as it had been during her first few days here back in March but colder because it was the middle of May now. The sounds and scents of the farm did their slow, gentle work, pushing the confronting pain of James's phone call a little further away.

She loved it here. She could happily breathe this air for the rest of her life.

Aunt Helen was over at the rotary clothesline, hanging out a load of linen and towels, fighting a billowing breeze. Kit crossed to her and began to help.

'Was that the phone?' her aunt asked.

'Yes, just a friend from Canberra, catching up on news.' She hid her face behind the damp towel she had begun to peg up.

'I can do this, love. Don't you have someone coming?'

'Emma. But I'm ready. We're going on a wine-tasting tour with a couple of her friends.'

Aunt Helen paused with her fingers holding a sheet in place and a peg pressed open. 'Really? An actual tour?'

'Yes, in a mini-bus, with a tour guide and a brochure. The works.' Kit grinned, appreciating her aunt's bemusement.

'Are they friends from out of town, then?'

'No.' Kit laughed. 'You look as if I've suddenly grown two extra heads.'

'Well, you know we always think of those things as being for tourists. You can stop in at Glen Aran any day of the week, never mind about a guide and a brochure.'

'Emma's idea. I think it'll be fun, actually. She feels as if she's in a bit of a rut, despite everything she's done on the house. I admire her for getting out and doing something about it... And here she is.'

'Have fun, love.'

'Planning to.' Aggressively planning to, after James's call, even if it meant she had to grit her teeth and force it every step of the way.

Emma was planning to have fun as well, it seemed. She had her unruly hair up in a twist on the top of her head, pearly eye make-up on her lids and a slash of lip gloss on her mouth. She looked good.

'Now, Kit, I'm not intending to get sloshed,' she said earnestly as she drove out to the road, 'But I *am* celebrating, so I hope you're in the mood to keep up.'

'Celebrating, Emma? Oh, what's happened?' The prospect of some good news was like the stab of a healthy appetite when good food was in view. Kit was impatient for it, hungry for it.

'You'll have to wait.' Emma gave a maddening smile. 'Nell and Caroline are meeting us at the information centre, but I'm not going to tell any of you until we've each got a glass in hand.'

When they reached the town's modern, airy tourist information centre, Emma made introductions. Kit hadn't met Caroline before—she worked in Glenfallon Hospital's pathology department—and knew Nell only as the rather formidable Dr Cassidy, head of the hospital's accident and emergency department. All four women were around the same age, give or take a couple of years.

Nell had a perfect figure, hidden beneath conservative casual clothes, and mouse-blonde hair looped back from her face with combs. Her eyes were a piercing blue, which could look like pure ice when she chose. Her mouth would have been full and sensual if she'd allowed it to be. Instead, unless she was speaking or smiling, she kept it firmly closed.

Dark-haired Caroline was warmer and far more maternal looking. A little overweight, too, although not as much as she apparently thought. She had an eleven-year-old son from a long-ended marriage, and he was with his grandparents this afternoon.

Kit was the new recruit in the group, the other three having been friends or neighbours on and off since school years spent together at GLC—Glenfallon's private girls' school.

The fourteen seater mini-bus was full, with a mix of tourists from several state capitals and from overseas and a guide-cum-driver who had obviously delivered his standard patter many times before.

'If we enjoy this, we should take a wine appreciation

course,' Caroline suggested. 'Not that I need—' She broke
off, glanced down at her well-padded figure and frowned.
'Actually, Weight Watchers is probably a better option in
my case.'

'So is learning not to obsess about it, Caro,' Nell said.

She was known in her department for these crisp lines,
and worse. Her nickname—IQ, short for Ice Queen—suggested both her bright mind and her cool temperament. Kit
wasn't sure what to think of her, but Caroline only smiled
at the comment, easily dismissing the barb in it.

'You're right of course,' she said.

'Wouldn't it be nice if it was as easy to fix your own
life as it is to give advice to your friends on how to fix
theirs?' Nell commented.

Both women laughed, and Kit relaxed a little. They were
obviously used to each other.

The mini-bus headed out of town, toward some vine-
covered hills several kilometres from Aunt Helen's farm,
and the driver announced that their first stop would be
Creston Estates, the district's biggest winery. It was a gra-
cious old place, and the tasting cellar was dark and cool.
Emma waited until all four women had a splash of golden
chablis in their glasses, then raised hers high.

'I'm taking three months of accrued leave, everyone,'
she announced. 'I'm blowing my savings, and I'm going to
Paris to learn to cook.'

Kit and Caroline both shrieked and exclaimed and started
asking questions. Nell drawled, 'I think you can get cooking lessons closer to home, Emma,' but no one took any
notice, and even Nell herself was smiling broadly.

'When?' Caroline demanded.

'Two weeks. I've been superstitious about it, and haven't
said a word. Didn't want to say anything until it was all
set in stone. Jane Cameron is coming back early from ma-

ternity leave, so she'll fill in for me. The real-estate agent thinks he's got a tenant for the house. I've booked my course, and I've rented a studio apartment that's about the size of a cardboard box, but I don't care, because I don't plan on being in it very much. So can someone please toast to the success of my adventure?'

To Kit's surprise, Nell was the one to oblige. She stepped forward, cleared her throat and came out with a clever little speech that made them all laugh. It had its usual sharp edge to it, however, and Kit found herself thinking, She's not happy. Even in the company of friends, she can't let go. I'm not surprised she has a reputation in her department…

But Nell gave Emma a warm hug, and the excitement was contagious. Aware of her own limited capacity for alcohol, Kit sipped cautiously at each wine, but it was hard to keep track of how much she'd had, and people kept saying to her, 'Did you try this one yet?'

She was relieved when the driver summoned them back to the bus…and not so relieved when he took a winding back road to their next scheduled stop—the Glen Aran winery across the road from Federica di Luzio's farm.

This time, they had a tour of the production facilities, which were filled with the powerful aroma of barrelled wine and the noise of machines at work. The tasting room was modern and bright with sunlight, and there was nowhere to sit down. The slight dizziness behind Kit's eyes turned into the sharpness of a headache, and her queasy stomach went out on strike in sympathy.

Emma hadn't noticed, and Kit didn't want her to. She deserved this afternoon of celebration and anticipation with her friends.

'*Vin blanc,*' she was saying, under the tutelage of winery owner Rick Steele, whom Kit remembered from dinner at Kingsford Mill with Gian, two months ago. '*Appellation contrôlée*. Is that right? I've been listening to lots of tapes. First time I've ever appreciated Madame Sauvage's teaching efforts at school. I've remembered more of it than I expected to. *Vin blanc. Cabernet sauvignon.* Try this one, Kit.'

'Mmm. OK.'

'Don't,' Nell said, snatching Kit's glass from her hand. 'Go outside. Now. Get some fresh air before it's too late.'

'Mmm.'

'Oh, Kit, has it gone to your head?' Emma was instantly remorseful and concerned.

''S OK.'

'Just leave her, Emma,' Nell said. 'Don't make her talk.'

Kit managed to get herself outside.

Just.

Fortunately, she was alone, and there were garden beds and orange trees and shade, and when she'd recovered—a little, not nearly enough—she found a water tank with a tap and could splash her face and rinse her mouth.

She was still crouching beside the gushing tap when she heard Gian Di Luzio's voice. 'Kit, what on earth…?'

She turned off the tap, straightened up and immediately felt her head pound as if it were cracking open, while the remaining contents of her stomach churned like a washing-machine. Gian was, at once, the person she least and most wanted to see in the whole world.

'Wine tasting,' she said. 'Not my thing…in the middle of the afternoon…as it turns out.'

She gave a watery smile.

'No, I can see it isn't,' he agreed bluntly. His black eyes studied her in detail. 'You're green.'

'Not surprised. Be kind, please, and tell me it's reflected light from the citrus leaves.'

'I will be kind.' His face softened, and he smiled. She

wanted to cry. And she wanted him to hold her. 'I'll run you across the road to the farm and tell my mother to find you some headache tablets and make you some tea. I've got the truck parked just around the corner.'

She opened her mouth.

'Planning to argue?' he asked, with a dangerous light in his eyes.

She shook her head.

'Good. Who should I tell?'

'Emma. Inside.'

'Come on. Here's the truck.' He helped her to the passenger seat, with a hand falling briefly here and there as he did so. On her shoulder, on her hip. If he was letting his touch linger a little longer than strictly necessary, she was still too ill to reach a definite conclusion on the issue. She sat in the truck, breathing very carefully, while he ducked back into the crowded tasting room.

'All fixed up,' he told her a few minutes later, then he drove, with a welcome attention to her fragile state, the short distance across the road and down the vine-and-rose-lined driveway to his mother's house.

Federica was in the big, sunny kitchen, mixing a cake, and her face lit up when she saw Kit. Gian forestalled a large, warm hug. 'Don't, Mum. She's feeling very fragile.'

'Wine tasting. Headache. Lost it,' Kit managed.

'There. Salient points covered in six words,' he said. 'I need to get back and finish our business with Rick. Mum will look after you, Kit.'

He touched her arm briefly, his fingers leaving a warm trail, and it was almost too much. Again, she could have cried. Or lost the final remnants of lunch.

'Poor thing,' Freddie said. 'And thank goodness Bonnie's having her nap, because you look too fragile to handle her hugs and shrieks at the moment. She's been asking if you could come over and draw some more fairies.'

It felt good to be fussed over by Gian's mother. Headache tablets, tea and dry biscuits. Solitude and silence on the couch. The cake went into the oven and began to fill the house with a sweet, lemony smell.

A little later, when Kit was feeling better, she went back into the kitchen, sat at the big wooden table and had a fresh-cut chunk of Italian bread topped with some sharp, crumbly cheese. The saltiness helped to settle her stomach, and the tablets had begun to take effect.

'Well, I'm never doing that again,' she said cheerfully, and heard Gian's laugh behind her as he opened the creaky screen door.

'Not "scrummy" this time?' he said.

The words and the tone arrowed straight into her heart. He remembered! It was two months ago now, but he remembered the exact, frivolous word she'd used to describe the wine at Kingsford Mill, and must remember, too, she was sure, the way they'd looked and smiled at each other that night.

She took a quick, unsteady breath and swivelled in her chair.

'Not at two-thirty in the afternoon,' she answered. 'I should have known. My body's just not made for it.'

'You're looking much better.' His dark eyes swept over her, taking inventory in a way that made her instantly hot. 'I told Emma I'd take you home.' The door creaked shut behind him, and he slid into a chair on the opposite side of the table, then reached for the round bread and the big knife.

'Thanks,' she answered, watching his hands.

His fingertips anchored the big loaf in place while he sawed back and forth with the knife, his rhythm practised and easy. The slice fell away from the loaf and he reached for the cheese, shaving it off thinly. Nothing extraordinary about any of it, but his actions soothed and warmed her. She ached to reach out and touch him, to discover whether his fingers were warm or cool today, to feel his caress on her skin.

It wasn't the first time she'd felt like this in recent weeks. Every time they encountered each other at work, she suffered through this same awareness, and had learned to be thankful for the fact that the pace was usually hectic when he was around.

She'd helped him to deliver a stillborn little girl. She had assisted with the vaginal delivery of a footling breech—a baby boy who'd turned in the womb just before the onset of a very rapid labour, leaving no time for the conservative approach of a Caesarean delivery.

She had encountered him on rounds during a two-week stint she'd spent in the postpartum side of the unit, and they'd met at the cafeteria and in the staff car park and in corridors and lifts.

This, though, was the first time in weeks that she'd seen him beyond the confines of the hospital, and the first time she'd seen him looking casual and relaxed in what was essentially his home.

Here, as she'd found during his brief appearance four weeks ago, it was much harder to ignore her awareness of him, and the silence between them was rapidly growing thicker. He was as relieved as she was, she sensed, when they heard a cry rising from the bedroom along the corridor.

'That's Bonnie waking up,' he said. 'Mum's outside. I'd better go.' He disappeared, calling to his little niece as he went. 'It's all right, Bonnie, love. Nonna's outside. Uncle Gian's here to pick you up. Come on, now.'

He was back in a few moments, with Bonnie in his arms.

She looked flushed and fretful. He went to the fridge and poured her some milk, one-handed, then returned to his bread and cheese and sat her on one thigh, with his spare arm wrapped around her little waist. She was beginning to settle now.

'Drink your milk, gorgeous,' he told her, and pressed a casual kiss to her dark little head.

He grinned at Kit and she smiled back, but she knew the smile fell away from her face too soon. She felt out of place, just *wrong* somehow. She shouldn't be here, when they'd agreed not to keep seeing each other, not to pretend friendship with each other, and when their reasons for making those agreements hadn't gone away, and never would.

She could imagine how they must look, grouped at the table over a simple snack.

Like a family.

One of them dark and one of them fair, with a little girl who took after her daddy.

But they weren't a family, of course. Gian didn't belong to Kit, and Bonnie didn't belong to either of them.

As if to emphasise this fact, Freddie came in through the back door at that moment, swung Bonnie up from her seat on Gian's thigh and said, 'I thought I heard you, sweetheart. That was a good big sleep, and now we'll never get you to bed tonight.'

'You could have left her, Mum,' Gian said mildly. 'She was quite happy where she was.'

'You took her shopping this morning. You need more time to yourself, Gian.'

'You do, too, Mum. You've been looking very tired, lately.'

Freddie ignored him. 'You need time to…' she glanced at Kit '…see friends. And relax. If Kit's feeling better— are you feeling better, Kit?'

Kit fell innocently into the trap at once, and said, 'Much, thanks.'

'Then you should take her round and show her the farm. Take her down to the creek.'

'You've seen the creek before, haven't you, Kit?' Gian said. 'It's the same one that runs through Helen's property.'

Before Kit could answer, Freddie cut in, 'Not *this* part of the creek. Take her. She'll appreciate the walk. And the fresh air.'

Gian's eyes met Kit's briefly. They both recognised that it was easier to accept than to argue.

'Sorry,' he said, as soon as they were safely outside.

'I like creeks. And fresh air.' And, heaven help her, she liked being with him, no matter how much she told herself that she shouldn't. There was an extra sweetness in the air, a lightness in her heart and a liquid warmth in her bones.

'You know what I mean.'

'Yes.' She laughed. 'Of course I do! Your mother's going to get the wrong idea.'

'Past tense, I think. She already has it. This is what I wanted to say, weeks ago, when you turned down coffee. Things like this will happen. I'm not sure how to handle it.'

'As friends, as far as everyone else is concerned? That works, doesn't it?'

'No.' Decisive, clipped, firm and not a hint of hesitation. 'It doesn't.'

She felt a little pang of anticipation, and a flutter of fear. He was striding away from the house, knowing exactly where he intended to go. To the creek, she guessed. Not because Federica had suggested it, and not because of her own insipid claim that she 'liked creeks'. It was because at the creek they could be alone.

Why hadn't she let him say it over coffee, that night when he wanted to? Coffee was public, and safe.

'It doesn't work, Kit,' he repeated. 'Not for me. And it's not how you wanted to handle it when we talked before.'

He strode on in silence down the dirt track that led away from the farmhouse, through the citrus grove, across a sheep paddock, over a rise and down to the rocky, eucalyptus-shaded creek. She had to walk at a rapid pace to keep up with him, and wondered if she'd have done better to take to her heels and sprint as hard as she could in the opposite direction.

'So,' Gian said as they cut through the dry grass of the creek bank and came down onto the big, water-smoothed stones. 'The creek.'

'We used to do all sorts of great things further upstream in this creek-bed when we came for holidays,' Kit said. 'It looks just the same.'

'We must have come close to meeting each other then,' Gian answered.

There was an old, fallen tree trunk lying in a dry section of the creek bed. It was iron-hard and silvery grey with age, warm and smooth in the sunshine like the well-fed belly of a huge horse. Gian rested one foot on the tree, and leaned his forearm across his knee.

'The friends thing,' he said. 'As far as I'm concerned, it's only possible if that's how two people actually feel. Pretending friendship is an uncomfortable thing to do. False. Dangerous.'

'I didn't mean we should pretend to each other,' Kit answered, her voice low. 'That's what I said before. I didn't want us to pretend to each other about any of this. But what choice is there as to how we behave in front of other people? Honesty can be dangerous, too. I couldn't bear for Freddie or Aunt Helen to know that we—that there *was* something we both felt, and that we had such unassailable reasons for deciding not to let it happen.'

'It's better, isn't it, than enduring their efforts to throw us together? How do we get them to stop? Those Italian mothers and Scottish aunts! You know they care about us. Let's tell them the truth.'

'No, Gian. I don't want to tell them about it.'

'I think you're wrong.'

'I couldn't stand to hear them assuring us that it didn't matter. People—kind people, who care—are often very good at telling those they love that problems don't matter, when actually they do.'

'I think you're wrong,' he repeated.

'It's my body, Gian.' Her voice was hard.

'And it's beautiful.' His voice was husky. 'I've tried, but I can't get over that. Your body is beautiful. And *you're* beautiful, Kit.'

He closed his thumb and forefinger in a ring around her wrist and slid them slowly up her arm. They both watched as the fine hairs there stood on end. He bent closer, shifted his weight, touched his fingers to her neck and brushed them along her jaw. She shuddered, and they both recognised that it was from pure need.

Whatever her mind might tell her, her body wanted this, and so did her heart. She felt the pressure of his thigh against her hip as he pulled her closer, and closed her eyes, as if that way she could pretend to both of them that his kiss would take her by surprise.

Stupid. Pointless.

She knew quite well that he was going to kiss her. There was no other reason for a man and a woman to stand this close. She could already feel the ridge of his arousal, and the insistent heat of his hard muscles beneath his smooth skin.

Her heart was hammering, and she began to melt inside. She waited for his kiss, but it didn't come.

'Look at me, Kit,' he whispered. 'Open your eyes.'

She did so, dragging lids that felt heavy and sleepy with wanting. He was watching her mouth with shadowed eyes, watching her lips part in expectancy and readiness, and his regard was so intense that it was almost as if he was touching her. He clearly intended to leave her with no room to doubt her own response, or his need.

Their kiss hung in the air while time slowed, slowed. His mouth was so close that she could feel his breath on the open fall of her lower lip. She chased him shamelessly, lifting her face, reaching up to anchor her hands in the prickly-soft hair of his nape, wanting desperately to consummate the moment of contact.

He laughed a little, the sound low and rich inside him, and his arms tightened around her, one hand flattened in a gesture of possession over the curve of her rear.

'See?' he said. 'See how much you want this, just the way I do?'

At last he touched her mouth, tasting her, claiming her for a moment, then drifting away once more.

'Oh!' she said.

He grinned, satisfied.

But then his control seemed to break, and suddenly he was crushing himself against her—mouth and chest and arms and thighs, leaving no room to breathe or speak or think, only what was needed for bare survival. Ragged breathing, snatched words, disjointed thinking.

Kit knew she should pull away, knew there were so many reasons why this shouldn't be happening, but somehow she couldn't remember any of them. In the two months since they'd agreed to turn their back on what they felt, and in the weeks since she'd pushed him away when he had tried to talk to her after the birth of Tracie McDowell's baby, none of it had gone away.

It had only strengthened. She was astonished at how much it had strengthened, when she'd only ever seen him in the course of their work, and during that one brief interlude at the farm.

She felt as if Gian Di Luzio had been in her life forever. Could barely remember a time when she hadn't listened for his voice when the phone rang in the unit, hadn't felt her heart quicken at the sound of his footsteps, hadn't known the way his eyelids creased when he was tired, or the way his voice seemed deeper pitched when he was called in to a delivery in the darkest hours of the night.

Still, this shouldn't be happening.

He slid his hands up beneath the stretch knit of her top, and traced the curve of her ribs with his fingers. He didn't touch her breasts, but she wanted him to. Her nipples hardened and stung with need, and she arched her back, aching for him to fill his hands with her weight.

She almost cried when he took his hands away, but then he began to peel her top upwards, pressed his mouth to her neck, her temple, her ear, and whispered, 'I want to see you. I don't want anything in the way.'

Slowly, she pulled the top over her head and felt the impatience in his fingers as he slid her bra straps down, twisted the fastening apart and dragged the garment from her arms. He groaned at the sight of her, and the fire in his dark eyes wrapped her in a swirl of female awareness.

Kit couldn't remember ever being desired like this, so nakedly, so hungrily. He wasn't afraid to show it, didn't care what she thought. He just wanted her, and it felt like a physical force, a molten flood of fire.

'Let me touch you?'

'Yes. Oh, yes.'

He brushed his hands lightly across her nipples, bent to kiss the valley between her breasts, deepened the valley by lifting her in his hands. She shivered, closed her eyes, folded her arms behind her neck and felt the warmth of the sun and of his mouth on her bare skin. His lips seared across hers once more, his hands captured her breasts briefly then came to rest at her waist.

'Now,' he said. 'Just try and tell me you don't want this. Try and tell me it isn't good. We've tried to step back and it hasn't worked. Nothing about what we first felt has gone away, and I'm tired—very tired, Kit—of the pretence.'

All at once, she felt tired, too.

And tricked.

She stepped out of the radiant heat of his hold on her and faced him, not troubling to hide the evidence of her desire. 'Did you hear what you just said, Gian?' Her voice was high. 'Nothing has gone away. Nothing has changed. The issue that made us agree to step back in the first place is still there, and it still matters.'

'Does it? Have we given ourselves a chance to find out if that's true?'

'It matters to *me*. There's nothing you can say. Nothing you can do. Not this...' She touched herself, brushing her palms across her peaked nipples, showing him what he'd done to her, knowing his body ached in just the same way. 'Not anything. I won't put myself through it again. I can't—' her voice cracked '—watch my infertility destroy another relationship, the way it destroyed what I had with James.'

Gian closed his eyes, and a shaft of four o'clock sunlight shone on his cheeks and his lashes. 'Put your clothes on,' he said harshly. 'We can't talk when all I can think of is the shape of you, and the way you feel.'

'We're not talking,' she answered, as she bent to retrieve

her bra and her top from beside the log where they had fallen. 'There's no need. I hate talking.'

He folded his arms across his chest, making the smooth muscles of his upper arms bulge and his forearms look like thick, braided rope. As she fiddled with the catch on her bra—her rubbery fingers wouldn't function—Kit watched his face, but it never moved. His mouth was pressed shut, his eyelids were thick and tanned and satiny over his eyes.

But perhaps he'd been listening to what she was doing, because as soon as she pulled her top down to meet her flowing skirt, he said, 'Done?' And opened his eyes.

'We're not talking,' she repeated.

'I want to hear about James.' His mouth was hard, and he'd narrowed his eyes. 'How long were you together before the problems started?'

'Three years.' She thought for a moment, and revised aloud, 'Two, really. I—Maybe I shouldn't have pushed him into trying for a baby when he didn't feel ready. His resentment started then, but he—No, he didn't try all that hard to hide it. I just didn't want to see it. I was so sure that if I could just conceive—'

'You think it was totally your fault, and you're taking on that same burden now. With us.'

'No. No, I'm not saying it was totally my fault.' She gave a harsh, jerky laugh. 'Believe me, the fact that James was sleeping with someone else behind my back is not something I'm taking on as my fault at all!'

He was silent, then he whistled. 'OK. Yes. That's a betrayal.'

'It was, yes. Gian, you deal with infertility, and with pregnancies and deliveries that go wrong. Babies who aren't perfect. I don't have to tell you what those kinds of problems sometimes do to people. I'm not going to do it to us.'

'Because "us" is important?'

'It could be,' she admitted. 'If we let it be.'

'How hard shall I fight you on this?' His tone was almost casual.

'Don't. Don't fight me on it at all. Let it go.'

'Then you should tell your aunt, and I should tell Freddie.'

'No.'

'You're leaving us in limbo. I know my mother. She had a light in her eyes just now when she suggested this little expedition. She's looking at the clock and timing how long we've been gone. She's not going to let go of this. She's not going to forget the vibe she picked up weeks ago—the vibe that's *there*, Kit, palpably there, and real, and important—unless she thinks we really don't like each other.'

'Then let her think that. *Make* her, and Aunt Helen, think that.'

'You honestly think that's an answer?'

'The best one we've got.'

He shook his head. 'If you make me any angrier, maybe you'll turn out to be right. Maybe it won't be so hard. You're wrong, Kit. I can't do it this way.'

She met his brooding gaze, and told him in a hard, steady voice, 'But I'm not offering you a choice.'

CHAPTER SEVEN

SOMEHOW, Kit and Gian made it back to the house.

Holding Bonnie's hand, Freddie wandered out from her vegetable garden, an expectant look ill-concealed on her face. 'Have you invited her to stay for dinner, Gian?'

'Not yet,' he growled. 'Do you want to stay for dinner, Kit?'

'Um, no, I should get home. I might walk. Just to make sure the headache doesn't come back.'

'There you are, Mum,' Gian said. 'She does this to everyone, Kit. No one ever escapes without the offer of a meal. It's an Italian thing.'

'It's nice,' she answered truthfully. 'But I can't, Freddie.'

'She sounds as if she means it, Mum, don't you think?' He had a dangerous look in his dark eyes, and a dangerous firmness to his mouth.

'You don't have to interpret me to your mother, Gian.' Kit's polite tone was strained. 'I think we speak the same language.'

Under the guise of walking her in the direction of the road, he murmured, 'Yes, but she's going to ask me, as soon as you've gone, why you're upset.' He brushed his knuckles softly against her neck and she couldn't help holding him, just gripping a fistful of his shirt fabric at the waist. His arm was warm against hers.

'I'm not upset,' she told him.

'Your cheeks have two spots of colour on them like pink coins. Your eyes are burning. And your top is crooked and not pulled down properly at the bottom...' He adjusted it as he spoke, his fingers lingering with deliberate intent. 'Which suggests I've been doing more than just upsetting you. What should I say?'

'That you made me angry, and I'm going home and she's not to get ideas.'

'I doubt that will be particularly effective.'

Bonnie was running after them, with Freddie coming up behind. Gian let Kit go and stepped back a pace. 'Do drawings?' the little girl asked Kit hopefully. 'Pincesses?'

'It's a conspiracy,' Kit muttered, adding aloud, 'Not today, love.'

'Kit's tired, sweetheart,' Freddie explained helpfully. 'She wants to be by herself. And I know how she feels.'

'Nonna draw pincesses?'

'Yes, Nonna can draw you some princesses.' Freddie sounded even wearier than Kit felt.

'Take a break tonight, Mum,' Gian said quietly. 'Go out.'

Freddie laughed. 'I'm too tired to go out. I want to stay home.'

'Then I'll take Bonnie to my place and we'll have a nice evening together. She'll stay the night. I'll even bring her to the office in the morning. Barb and Margaret will look after her until you can get into town to pick her up. Take it easy for once, and sleep in.'

'She'll wake in the night.'

'I know. But I'm used to disrupted nights. And you need a night when you can go to bed knowing you won't be disturbed.'

Freddie turned to Kit with a hesitant, hopeful expression. 'Kit, maybe—'

'If you're planning to ask Kit to help me, please don't,' Gian said firmly.

'Well…'

'You're too old-fashioned, Mum. Just because I have a

Y chromosome, that doesn't mean I can't handle a toddler on my own. Bonnie and I will be fine, and we'll do this more often in future. It's not enough for me just to come out to the farm for an hour or two, here and there. You need a complete break. I'm going to talk to Marco, too, about other solutions, long term.'

'Toddlers are always difficult.'

'Which is why nature usually arranges it so that women in their mid-sixties don't have to handle them full time.'

'Kit…' Freddie began again. This time Gian let her finish. 'I'm sorry,' she said. 'We're treating you like family, dealing with all this in front of you.'

'It's nice to be treated like family,' Kit answered without thinking, and knew at once that she'd just deepened the hole she was so determined not to fall into.

'It's really over this time,' Pete Croft told Gian.

His surgery was in the same building as Gian's—part of a two-storey complex of professional offices and small shops a couple of blocks behind Glenfallon's main shopping streets. The two of them were on opposite sides of an open stairwell, and Pete had become a quasi-friend over the past couple of years, and not only due to the proximity of their offices.

It was the kind of friendship that men tended to create—cordial and supportive, even though they rarely touched on personal issues and mostly stuck to sport and politics and professional matters, over the occasional drink.

It had been hard to avoid the personal issues today, however. Claire had shown up while Pete was seeing his last patient of the day, gunning her car engine and jumping the kerb outside his office. She'd narrowly escaped mowing down a young tree, then had parked illegally with the car's nose jutting onto the tiled walkway that led to the stairs.

She'd unloaded several boxes of files, papers and journals which Pete must have had at home, and she'd banged the car boot lid, and the passenger door, and the door to Pete's waiting room so emphatically each time that Gian couldn't concentrate on the notes he was dictating into his tiny hand-held recorder. He'd given up and sat in his chair, watching Claire go back and forth until she was done.

She was an attractive woman, with a good figure and a bell of dark, glossy and well-cut hair swinging around her face. It was a tight face, though, with a mouth that was usually folded in at the corners, and she rarely smiled.

Pete had come over several minutes later to apologise for the whole scene, and Gian had suggested, 'You might appreciate a beer.'

'Not in public, thanks. I'd kill for a quiet one in here.'

Gian's receptionist, Barb, had still been in the file room, finishing up for the day. She'd heard Claire's activity as well. Gian had sent her down the block to the nearest bottle shop for a six-pack of chilled cans. Pete had drunk half of one can before speaking anything more than the odd terse word.

'What are you going to do?' Gian asked him now.

'I'm in a motel for the moment. I've got a real-estate agent who thinks he has a place that would suit me until I can get things sorted out more permanently.' He took another gulp of his beer. 'I wanted to make this work. For the girls' sake, really.'

'Is that a good enough reason?'

'No. It isn't. It wasn't. It might have been, if Claire had met me halfway. But when a woman is, to all intents and purposes, standing there with her arms folded, saying in a dozen different ways each day, Prove to me why I should love you, or even why she should *like* me, and chalking up every tiny fault and mistake and habit as damning reasons

why she shouldn't...' He trailed off and shook his head.
'You just can't win in that situation.'

Gian didn't know what to say. Didn't want to bring up
his own divorce as proof that life went on after it was all
over, because he wasn't particularly happy with his life in
that area at the moment. Kit McConnell was well and truly
stuck under his skin, and he saw her at just the right tan-
talising frequency to keep his feelings frozen in a state of
simmering limbo.

The tension was building, however. The balance between
hope and hopelessness was shifting. If he went on feeling
this way for much longer, he knew he was going to confront her again, but he still didn't know how it would resolve itself. He was already afraid that her doubts ran too
deep, and that he'd say something he would later regret.

Didn't want to make the same mistake with Pete.

'It sounds as if you've done the right thing,' he said to
the other man cautiously. 'Sounds as if you should give
yourself some time before you commit yourself to any big
decisions.'

'My main concern is the girls. I just want to keep things
as smooth as possible for their sake.'

'Kids are a bit of a compass, I guess.'

'That's a good way to put it. They keep you pointed in
the right direction.'

Pete finished his beer a few minutes later. Gian gave him
the rest of the six-pack to take back to his solitary motel
room, but he himself took away a less concrete yet potentially more valuable remnant from their conversation—the
image of children as a compass 'keeping you pointed in
the right direction'.

He sat for several minutes at his desk, then reached for
the phone and keyed a long series of numbers. After one
ring, his call was picked up at the other end, and he said,

'Could I speak to Marco Di Luzio, please? This is his brother phoning from Australia.'

When the call was put through, he didn't spend more than a minute on the niceties of greetings and enquiries as to health. Instead, he got to the point of his call as quickly as he could. 'We need to make a better arrangement about Bonnie,' he told his younger brother. 'I really think you should come home, to see her and to talk, as soon as you can. If you're ever going to have her with you, then you have to do it soon.'

'Gian—'

'And if you're not, then we need to talk about the alternatives.'

Emma went to Paris.

Bringing Kit and Nell and Caroline together for a final coffee at the Glenfallon Bakery two days before she left, she told them that her tenant, for the next three months, was Pete Croft. His reconciliation with Claire hadn't lasted, and he was on his own again.

He'd jumped at Emma's house, apparently, because the short lease gave him the right window in which to make long-term plans for his future. All indications were that this time the separation from his wife was final, and should perhaps have happened long before. Emma's place was close to the house he owned with Claire, which would allow him easy and frequent contact with his four-year-old twin daughters.

'I hope it works out for him,' Emma said. 'For me, of course, he's an ideal tenant. Responsible and steady. I was a little concerned about renting the house out, right after all the work I've done on it, but I really needed to. As it is, I'm not sure what Dad would have thought of me spending so much of what I've saved over the years on a jaunt like this.'

'I envy you, Emma,' Nell said. 'Don't give another thought to the money. Seriously. You need this. And we don't all get what we need, when we need it. I'm sorry, that's too profound for today.' She smiled her complicated smile. 'Just…have fun.'

Kit missed Emma when she had gone. They'd had a lot in common, not just in terms of where they each found themselves in life—at a crossroads, ready for change—but in terms of their outlook as well.

Caroline and Nell could have become friends with Emma's presence to smooth the way, but Kit felt that she didn't know them well enough yet to cement a friendship with them on her own. She was a little daunted, too, by Nell's senior position at the hospital, which Nell herself tended to hide behind when she wanted to. She'd only nodded curtly at Kit during the few times they'd encountered each other at work since the wine-tasting afternoon.

Jane Cameron, Emma's replacement, was competent and friendly, and still a little torn between wanting to work and wanting to spend time with her little son, aged nine months.

'I hope I'm doing the right thing, coming back,' she said. 'I need to, financially, or we won't be able to afford to have another one, but I wonder if I'm short-changing him. At least we don't depend on full-time child-care. Len has him for a lot of my hours, and so does Mum. Take notes, you guys,' she lectured Kit and Maree and Alison. They were gathered for the hand-over report. 'Because your turn will come, and it isn't easy!'

Kit smiled and nodded, just like the other two, and was glad that Gian wasn't in the unit right now. He would have known too much about what she was hiding.

He arrived five minutes later, to check on a private patient—a first-time mother—whose labour was progressing very slowly. Kit was re-equipping a resus trolley, since its previous occupant had graduated to breathing room air and was now snuggling safely in his mother's arms.

She didn't hear Gian behind her, but he was still in her thoughts and she jumped when she heard his voice. 'Kit, which room is Jodie Bambridge in?'

She rounded on him, her hand fisted over her heart, and spoke bluntly. 'Do you have to do that? Some people say hello first.'

'Sorry, I'm in a hurry.' Even such a brief, casual sentence seemed to pour sensation down her spine like someone pouring a cup of warm cream.

'Room Three,' she answered. 'It's on the board.'

'Next time, I'll check the board.'

'That's why it's there.'

She didn't care that she'd angered him, or slighted his rank. All their exchanges contained this underlying vein of tension, the pull of fiery awareness and unresolved conflict, and she hated the fact that he dominated her thoughts so much. Stripping the resus trolley's tiny, plastic-covered mattress, she fitted a clean sheet, muttering, 'Go away, Gian. Just go away.'

'Hell, Kit!' His voice came from just a few feet away, and it was obvious that he'd heard.

'I—I didn't mean you,' she said.

'You said my name.'

She looked up at him, and her heart flipped as usual. He was wearing snug-fitting green surgical gear. There was no stretch in the fabric, and it sat closely against his strong, olive-brown chest. He was like a magnet to her senses, unravelling them strand by strand and reeling them in. 'I was telling you to get out of my thoughts,' she said.

A dangerous light had appeared in his dark eyes,

screened just a little by his thick lashes. 'And will I listen?' he asked.

'You don't generally. You're very persistent. And slow to take a hint. You hang round where you're not wanted and just refuse to leave. In my thoughts, I mean.'

'Maybe there's a reason for that, which you're not admitting to.' He left her no time to even consider the comment, let alone reply to it. 'Now, Jodie Bambridge.'

'Room Three,' she reminded him.

'Yes. Has she been walking around?'

'No, we've tried—suggested it and pushed a little—but she didn't want to.'

'Thanks. That's all I wanted to know.'

This time, she watched to make sure he'd really gone to his patient's room, and when he disappeared, she muttered once more, 'Go away, Gian.'

He didn't. Or at any rate, not for long. Hardly his fault tonight. They had a new admission who was consigned to Kit's care at eight o'clock. Although the patient was only twenty-seven, this was her fifth baby and her seventh pregnancy, and her history was a litany of obstetric problems. Kit knew from the beginning that this new baby was going to continue the pattern.

Sandy blonde Belinda Carter was very slight around the hips. She was in established labour, but the baby was two weeks early, was lying sideways and didn't feel as if it was intending to move. Belinda had come in alone—'My sister dropped me off'—and she looked tense, with red-rimmed eyes.

'I'd like to get you to walk around,' Kit suggested, 'because that might help shift the baby into a better position. Can you do that?'

'Sure. It's not hurting that much. And I need to make

some calls.' She dragged a mobile phone from the back pocket of her maternity jeans and flipped it open.

'We have a public phone at the end of the corridor,' Kit told her. 'You can't use your mobile in the hospital, because the signal can interfere with our equipment.'

'Oh, is that right? OK.' She shrugged. 'Just as long as I can call. My husband got arrested tonight, the silly galah, and I need to get him bailed out so he can come and hold my hand!'

She laughed. It was a rich, warm sound which invited Kit to share in her unlikely source of amusement, and her freckle-dappled nose wrinkled, making her look like a mischievous little boy.

Then she caught sight of Kit's face.

'Oh, it's all right!' she said. 'He just got into a fight outside the pub. They're best mates, really. I was standing right there, trying to pull them apart, when the police showed up, and Travis got a bloody nose, and my waters broke, boom, boom, boom, just like that, everything at once.'

'Is that why you looked a bit upset when you came in?'

'Well, yes, I was mad at him. Wouldn't anyone be? But I'm OK now. Travis and Brett are both going to feel sorry for themselves in the morning, and I won't spare either of them any sympathy!' She laughed again. 'Meanwhile, Travis can come and hold my hand, even if he'd rather be holding his own head. Only I need to ring around and see who's got the bail money to lend us!'

She sat on the edge of the bed, waiting out a contraction with stoical patience. All she did was mutter, 'Ouch! I remember now. I don't like this part, do I?'

When the pain had ebbed, she went along the corridor to the phone and made her calls. She returned, smiling. 'I love my brother! He's meeting Travis at the cop shop with the cash. Contractions aren't speeding up nearly as fast as they did last time. Feels funny. I think the baby's still sideways.'

Kit checked, and it was. She got Belinda to rest on all fours on the bed through several contractions, and attempted an external manipulation, but the baby wouldn't budge. From the feel of the limbs, head and spine, it was well and truly wedged, but babies did flip, *in utero*, at the most unexpected times.

She checked the heartbeat, which was strong, and the colour of the amniotic fluid, which was clear. They could wait a while yet.

Travis Carter arrived an hour later, agitated and smelling of beer. 'I'm in time, then?'

'Yes, and very welcome, I think!' Kit told him.

His wife's contractions were becoming more frequent, and more intense. The baby had stayed exactly where it was. Belinda was very good about shuffling up and down the corridor, trying to help things along, but the baby still wouldn't turn.

After making quite sure that Belinda and her husband were speaking to each other in amicable terms, given the story about the fight outside the pub, Kit headed towards the nurses' station and met Gian's private patient shuffling in the opposite direction. Gian had satisfied himself that she was doing fine, and had left some time ago.

Jodie looked tired and discouraged now, but then a contraction came, gripping her powerfully. After it was over, she said, 'I think the baby's dropped. I can breathe. Maybe something's happening after all.'

For Belinda, something certainly was. 'This is getting really, *really* annoying!' she gasped. 'It hasn't turned, has it?'

'No, it hasn't,' Kit agreed. 'I think you're going to need

some help getting this one out, Belinda. You'll have to have a Caesarean.'

'Well, I'm used to problems,' she sighed. 'At least it's not three months early, like Savannah was, when I was eighteen.'

Gian appeared when Belinda was already prepped for a Caesarean delivery, and Clive was on hand to give her epidural anaesthesia. Kit filled Gian in quickly and quietly on the patient's background and her previous six pregnancies.

Abortion, premature delivery, premature delivery, miscarriage, stillbirth, postpartum haemorrhage…and this time, as well as a baby stuck in a transverse lie, Belinda had a husband bailed out from the lock-up after a boozy pub fight, just in time to get here for the delivery.

Gian raised his eyebrows, and Kit murmured, 'I know. But she seems terrific, actually. She's taking it all in her stride, barely complaining about the pain, resigned to another difficult delivery. Laughing about anything she can find that's remotely funny. And the husband looks embarrassed, as if he knows he's stuffed up. I think they'll be OK.'

'Hope so.' He'd had his head bent towards her to hear her murmured words, but now he straightened, robbing her of the aura of his warmth.

Jane took Travis away to the little waiting room along the corridor, between the obstetric operating theatre and the main part of the unit, where he could chew on his nails, drink coffee and pretend to watch TV. He hadn't wanted to be present during his wife's surgery, although it was permitted when a patient was having epidural anaesthesia.

'Oh, well,' Belinda said. 'Never mind. He hates blood.'

She must have been in enormous discomfort, because the baby's position was horrendous, imprisoned by her slight frame. His head and shoulder were wedged under her ribs and his spine was curved down into her pelvic cavity, with feet and hands tangled in a knot in the middle. She didn't complain, however.

Gian used the standard low transverse incision, and managed to manoeuvre him out feet first, but not without Kit's assistance, providing pressure and pull when instructed. Working so closely together, they touched from time to time. His hip nudged her side, or his elbow brushed across her forearm. She steeled herself to ignore the moments of contact, but wasn't always successful. She noticed he was frowning.

Fortunately, it was all over quite quickly.

'A boy!' Belinda exclaimed. 'Oh, that's great! After three girls! Travis is going to be totally rapt!'

He was.

Kit took the baby out to him while his wife was still being stitched up, and he swallowed and grinned and blinked back tears. He had ears that stuck out like jug handles and hair like a bristly brown dog. But his eyes were a warm, friendly blue and he obviously knew what love meant.

He could hardly speak as he looked at his little boy. 'Can I...? Mum's here. Can I take him out and...?'

'That should be all right,' she told him.

The baby was healthy and alert, small but strong. The waiting room was just down the corridor. There was no reason to say no.

'But don't be long,' Kit added. 'You'll be able to go in to see Belinda as soon as she's in Recovery.'

Kit gave him the tiny bundle and walked with him to the waiting room, where she saw an older woman, a man who was probably Travis's father and a younger man and woman who might have been a brother and sister.

She went back to the nurses' station to fill in Belinda's

notes, then had to field a couple of phone calls. One was from a woman at around the thirty-fifth week of pregnancy, whose feet had swollen. Should she come in? Was it dangerous? Kit asked some questions which satisfied her that the situation wasn't urgent, gave her some advice and suggested a visit to the pre-natal clinic tomorrow.

The second call was from Jodie Bambridge's mother, asking if there was any news. As yet, there wasn't, although David Bambridge and midwife Alison Kiel were coaching her through some long, intense and frequent contractions now. Jodie's mother was persistent, however, wanting details and time-frames that Kit couldn't provide with any accuracy. It took her longer than she would have liked to deal with the call.

While she listened to Jodie's mother, she saw one of Travis Carter's relatives appear from along the corridor. He looked around for a few seconds, then went back the way he'd come, and she heard voices. She didn't think anything of it at the time.

She was just about to go back to her patient, planning to collect the baby boy from his dad on the way, when Gian appeared. He looked tired around the eyes, and his hair was rumpled now that he'd removed his cap.

'Where's the baby?' He massaged a tight spot at the back of his neck with fingers and thumb.

'You just passed him, didn't you? In the waiting room with several relatives.'

'There's no one in there. Belinda is in Recovery now, and she wants him. And her husband. And I'd like to grab a break before Jodie's ready to deliver, so—'

'Yes, go then,' she invited him. 'I'll chase the baby. I'm sure he can't have gone far.'

'Belinda was getting anxious.'

'There were a couple of calls.' She glanced at the clock

on the opposite wall. 'I'm sorry. You're right. I didn't intend to be away this long.'

'That's fine. You're doing your job. Hannah is still clearing up in Theatre, and Maree is looking after Belinda in Recovery. Just produce that baby!'

But Kit couldn't.

Gian was right. There was no one in the waiting room. She went along to the obstetric operating theatre and adjoining recovery annexe, but encountered no one. Maree was talking to Hannah Ward, propping the Theatre door open with her shoulder. Belinda struggled to sit up in the bed as soon as she saw Kit, but her legs were still immobilised from her recent anaesthesia and she couldn't move. This added at once to her anxiety.

'Have you got him?' she demanded. 'Where is he?'

'Your husband has him, Belinda, but for the moment I don't know where they've—'

'Was his mother there?' Belinda cut in. 'Has his mum come in?'

'I think so.'

Belinda swore. 'That woman! She's always hated me. She's taken him. She's got Travis to kidnap my baby. Why did you let him take him?' Her voice rose almost to a shriek.

Kit's stomach became a stone inside her, heavy and hard. She remembered the male Carter relative surveying the unit before disappearing back along the corridor, and the sound of voices, no longer coming from inside the waiting room but from the corridor itself. In the space of a few minutes, her innocent gesture of letting a proud dad take his new son out to show the grandparents had become potentially the biggest mistake of her career.

'Don't worry, Belinda, I'm sure he'll be all right,' she said automatically. 'I'll check. I'll be back.'

Her voice seemed to come to her own ears from a long way away, sounding hollow, and she knew she must be white to the lips. On paper legs, she went back along the corridor to the main part of the unit. The waiting room was still empty. In Room Three, Jodie was moaning, almost drowning the sound of Alison's reassuring voice. Gian stood in the unit kitchen, drinking coffee. The fresh smell of it made Kit queasy.

'Everything OK?' he asked, as soon as he saw her.

'No, it's not.' Her voice was still strange, and she saw Gian's eyes narrow at once. 'The baby's gone. The Carter baby.' She tried to remain calm. 'Or Belinda thinks he has.'

'Gone?'

'Taken. Kidnapped.'

'That's ridiculous.' He set his mug on the counter top with an abrupt thud. 'Let me talk to the mother.'

But Belinda was almost hysterical when they got back to her. Hannah was with her, trying to calm her down by getting a list of phone number they could try to see if Travis and the baby were there. If Travis had taken him, where might they have gone?

As soon as Belinda saw Kit, she turned on her. 'How could you do this? How could you just give him my baby and let him walk out?'

'I didn't see any of them go past, Belinda. I—'

'If something happens to him…'

Yes, it was Kit's worst nightmare, too. She tried to rationalise. Travis had obviously been entranced by his new son. He wouldn't intentionally harm the baby. Although on the small side, just over six pounds, the little boy had seemed robust. He was warmly wrapped, with a stretchy hat on his head to keep the heat in, and most newborns didn't need to feed immediately.

'I'll make you miserable for the rest of your life!' Belinda yelled.

'Mrs Carter!' Gian's voice was rigid with authority. 'I cannot allow you to terrorise the nursing staff.' But his black eyes glittered coldly as he glanced at Kit, and she knew he was angry. He thought she'd mishandled this, misread the signs, and evidently he was right.

'Let's take this calmly, shall we?' he went on. 'I'll call hospital security, and they'll contact the police. We'll get people working on this immediately. If your relationship with your husband is that combative, Mrs Carter, you should have told us.'

'It's not,' Belinda sobbed. 'It's not combative. Most of the time. It's just his mother. She's a dragon, and she can get him to do anything she wants. I don't know why he listens to her. She always said I was an unfit mother, and someone should take the kids away, and now she's done it. I know she has!'

Gian went to a wall phone and pressed the three digit code that connected him to Security.

'We've got a major incident,' he said. His dark, flickering gaze swept over Kit, then moved on. 'Can you come up straight away? And we'll need the police as well.' He listened for a moment, then suggested, 'The patient conference room in the maternity unit. Would that work?' He put his hand over the receiver and turned back to Belinda. 'Is there any chance that the baby is in physical danger, Mrs Carter?'

'Travis would never hurt him, I know that. But he's a newborn. He's so tiny, and he hasn't been fed.'

A minute later, Gian and Kit were once again heading back along the corridor. Gian's demeanour was icy, while Kit flamed with remorse. How could this be happening?

Gian evidently wondered the same thing. 'For heaven's

sake, Kit, didn't you sense that the family situation was unstable?' He spoke with a quiet intensity that chilled her.

'No, I didn't,' she retorted. 'I filled you in on it, remember? A little chaotic, for sure, with tragedy and farce all mixed in together, but they seemed all right. They seemed to love each other. When I handed Travis the baby, he was beaming and he had tears in his eyes. I can't believe they've just disappeared.'

'You'd better start to believe it, and to take it seriously.'

'Of course. I didn't mean—It's just an expression, Gian.'

Her voice cracked. She desperately wanted just a few words from him, a tiny concession. That he might have done the same thing in the same situation. That this had come from left field, and that it wasn't her fault. Most of all, that he was sure the newborn baby would be recovered soon, and with no ill effects.

But he didn't give an inch. 'Even if the baby is recovered quickly, this is going to trigger a full review of unit procedures and policy. It's going to be a nightmare, Kit.'

'Are you laying it all on me?' She would have been angry if she hadn't been too upset. The underlying tension and the unresolved issues between them had flared, heating the space between them to combustion point.

'Of course I'm not!' he snapped. 'But it's another instance of the nursing staff wanting everything in the unit to be warm and fuzzy, even if that means ignoring more important issues. Laura Madigan's baby, a few months ago, nearly suffered permanent damage as a result of the same thinking.'

'That's incredibly unfair!'

'Life isn't fair, Kit,' he answered heavily. 'Don't you know that by now?'

They both heard voices coming from the waiting room

at that moment. Gian looked at Kit. 'What the—? Is that Jodie's family?'

'I don't think so. I had her mother on the phone earlier, and I don't think she was planning to come in until—'

He didn't wait for her to finish but took three strides ahead of her and swung himself around the open doorway first, the muscles of his forearm hard and ropy as he grabbed the frame. She was right behind him. In the waiting room, Travis held his newborn son, while his parents and siblings looked on. All of them were smiling and talking, without an apparent care in the world. They smelled strongly of cigarette smoke.

'We have quite a search party gearing up to look for you and your baby son, Mr Carter,' Gian said. Kit recognised at once that his calm tone was pure façade. 'Where have you been?'

Travis looked blank. 'Down in the car park, having a smoke.'

'You didn't tell anyone where you were going, and no one saw you leave. How did you get out?'

'Down the fire stairs, on the way to the operating room. We didn't disturb any patients that way, and it was quicker than coming out to the lift.' He frowned. 'There isn't a problem, is there? Can I see Belinda yet?'

'Yes, you can see her. In fact, she's been waiting for a while, and she's somewhat upset. If you'll excuse me, I have an important phone call to make. Kit, maybe you could handle this now?' His tone was suspiciously thready.

'I thought I wasn't to be trusted,' she muttered to him, still furious and weak with reaction.

'You've had a reprieve,' he muttered back. 'And if I can call off Security within the next thirty seconds, there's a chance we may be able to keep the lid on this fiasco after all.'

'Thanks for your support.' Her hard, sarcastic drawl wobbled, despite her best efforts. 'All I care about, right now, is the fact that the baby's safe.'

'This isn't personal, Kit,' he rasped.

'Isn't it? It is for me.'

A beat of silence emptied the air, and then he answered, 'Then we'd better talk, as soon as we get a chance.'

He'd left the room before she could find a reply.

Back in Recovery, Belinda burst into tears of relief as soon as she saw Travis and the baby. 'What's this all about, you crazy woman?' he asked her tenderly.

'Well, I knew you weren't quite sober. And I know your mum didn't think we should have had him in the first place. When they couldn't find you, I got it in my head you must have taken him away. To your sister, or somewhere. To your mum's family in Queensland. I just panicked.'

'It's all OK now.'

'Kid's already causing trouble and he isn't even an hour old.' Belinda gave a wobbly laugh. 'We'd better think of a name for him.'

Kit didn't agree with Travis that 'it was all OK now'. Neither, obviously, did Gian. He was still hanging around the unit when she was ready to go off at eleven, as Jodie was in transitional stage labour and almost ready to push.

'I'll phone you,' Gian told Kit, and it sounded like a threat. 'Tomorrow.'

She just nodded, and hoped no one else had heard. Jane, Deanna and Juliet were gathering for the hand-over report, and it would be a quick one with Jodie's delivery so close.

'We had some drama,' Jane announced to the incoming midwives. She summarised the false alarm over the Carter baby's disappearance in three sentences, then said, 'Dr Di Luzio wants us to keep it very quiet. There'll be some follow-up.'

'Even though it was all a mistake?' Deanna Fields asked.

'Yes, because next time it might not be. We'll have to review our policies regarding security and access, and the status of those fire stairs. But Dr Di Luzio doesn't want the higher echelons of management involved at this stage. Not until we've got some solutions to propose. And he definitely doesn't want the story going beyond the hospital.'

'Are you all right about it, Kit?' Julie Wong asked. 'You look so flushed.'

'It wasn't fun at the time. I don't think my heart's back in the right place in my chest yet.'

'Did Dr Di Luzio blame you for the mix-up?'

'More or less.'

'He's usually more open-minded than that. Conservative in a lot of ways, but still he's usually great.'

'He's right.' Why was she defending him? she wondered. He'd been far more unpleasant than he'd needed to be. 'There were some signs which should have had me keeping a better eye on parents and baby.'

Kit escaped a few minutes later, before anyone had a chance to question her more closely.

CHAPTER EIGHT

'I'M SORRY, Kit.' Gian's voice rumbled low and husky in his chest, and his arms wrapped around her while she was still struggling to remember how to breathe. 'That's really all I can say. I'm just…sorry. I was tired, and tense, with a whole lot of stuff on my mind, and—No excuses. I'm just sorry.'

He'd hardly said anything on the phone an hour ago, just after breakfast. He'd simply given her the address of his unit in town and asked if she was free to meet him there this morning. She was, although she'd been tempted for a moment to make up an excuse. The clipped quality to their conversation suggested that he was still angry.

But just now, when he'd opened the door to her jittery presence…

'It's all right,' she answered, her voice muffled against his shirt, because as soon as she was in his arms like this, hearing his low, emotional voice, it was the truth. Against all logic, everything was all right now.

He felt so warm and solid and male. His shirt smelled of eucalyptus detergent and sunshine, and his neck of coffee and sweet soap. His jaw pressed against her hair, and their legs tangled together, length to length. She couldn't remember anything ever feeling this *right* before.

'We won't be alone for long,' he said. 'I'm sorry about that, too. Mum's dropping Bonnie over. I wanted to see you, and I didn't want to say no to her, since she so rarely suggests it. I hope that's all right.'

'Of course it is. I love Bonnie. And I wanted to see you, too.'

'I'm so sorry about last night.' He brushed his cheek against hers like a big cat, and she felt the corner of his mouth as it crossed hers. She wanted to capture it, keep it, kiss it.

'It was a scare for all of us,' she said.

'And it wasn't your fault. I should never have suggested that it was. We need a better policy in place. The chances of something like that happening for real have increased in recent years, with more complex blended families and some disaffected non-custodial fathers.'

'A mother will usually alert us to that sort of situation, and disaffected fathers aren't usually a loving presence during the birth. That's why I never thought, last night—'

'One day, a woman might not be in a fit state to think of it. I lay awake half the night thinking about this.'

'So did I,' she muttered. 'And I thought about you.'

'Hell, Kit!' He pressed his lips to her temples, her cheeks, her mouth, then pulled back a tiny bit. 'You shouldn't have.'

'How could I help it?'

'I'm going to suggest we put a silent alarm on the door to the fire stairs—one that lights up at the nurses' station and perhaps in Security as well. With the new obstetric theatre at the end of the corridor, we're getting patients and visitors aware of that fire door when they didn't used to be, because they never went that far along. It's an emergency exit and it should be marked that way. We can't have it used for everyday comings and goings. We're asking for trouble.'

'That's all very well, Gian. I mean, it's good. It seems like a solution. But why were you so angry last night? I—I couldn't understand it. And it hurt.'

'Because I need you in my life.' He held her once more, raked his fingers through her hair and along her jaw. 'That doesn't make sense, I guess. Not logical at all, and not particularly admirable, but it's the reason.'

The ball of his thumb brushed her lips, and his eyes were like black pools.

'This isn't going to go away until we do something about it,' he went on softly, and she couldn't take her eyes from his face. 'We've tried to pull back and it hasn't worked, hasn't changed how we feel.'

'No…'

'I want us to be lovers. I don't want to decide *now* what might eventually break us apart. A hundred other issues could end up doing that, without us ever getting to whether we can have a baby together or not. I want to take a risk, Kit. I want us to have something *now*.'

'Me, too,' she whispered. 'You're right. It's too hard to keep saying no to this.'

The last three words were lost against his mouth, and he kissed her until she was dizzy and heavy and melting and weak. She had to hold onto him for support, and to orient herself in space, and for the moment, nothing else existed but this.

'When is Bonnie coming?' she managed at last.

'About now, probably.' His eyes swam with dark, liquid heat. 'Have to say, at the moment I wish she wasn't. I can think of other ways I'd rather spend the day, involving just the two of us. Are you working tonight?'

'No, not until Monday.'

'I'm on call from six for run-of-the-mill emergencies, and any time for extra serious ones. Hopefully there won't be any of those.'

'There aren't any very often, are there?'

'Not often, especially since Pete Croft came back from

Sydney, with his obstetric and neonatal care qualifications upgraded. Mum always knows there's a chance she might have to collect Bonnie again in a hurry. I'm not sure that wanting to spend the day in bed with you is an excuse I want to use for reneging on the arrangement, though. She already drops your name into the conversation far too often. Oh, damn, here she is.'

They both heard the car pull up just outside, and the sound of Bonnie's voice in mid-chatter as soon as the car door opened.

'Here's a kiss you owe me for later, with interest,' Gian said softly, and the touch of his mouth had come and gone before Kit had even tasted it. She was left with closed eyes, a trembling mouth and a deep hunger inside her which she knew he shared.

If Federica wondered why Kit was here, she was tactful enough not let it show. She had a stream of instructions and suggestions for Gian, and he listened to all of them patiently.

'OK, now it's my turn,' he said when she'd finished. 'Go to a matinée movie. I've looked in the paper, and there are two things showing that you should like. Have lunch in town, buy yourself some new clothes, go home and take a nap, and I'll deliver Bonnie back for dinner.'

'Will you stay for dinner, Kit?' Freddie asked.

'I didn't say that *I'd* stay for dinner, Mum,' Gian pointed out.

She tilted her chin up, and gave him a wicked, sideways look. 'Maybe I'm just inviting Kit.'

He laughed. 'Don't cook. We'll get Chinese or something, and leave ourselves flexible.'

When Freddie had gone and Bonnie was busy unpacking the entire contents of the bag of child equipment her grandmother had brought, Kit said, 'Your mother's definitely going to get ideas.'

'Oh, to hell with it, she can have them!' he answered, and the look he gave her stole the breath from her lungs. 'As many ideas as she wants.'

She couldn't argue, even though she felt that she probably should.

They had a wonderful day, and Kit hoped that Freddie was having one, too. She had looked wrung out, and Gian was right to bully her a little, if it meant she would take the breaks she needed.

They took Bonnie to the local playground, where she was happy for Gian and Kit to take turns pushing her in the rubber-seated swing until they'd both had a thorough upper body workout. She loved the slide, too, which seemed extra slippery today with the sun dazzling on its metal surface. They ate muesli bars and drank juice in boxes for a morning snack, and Bonnie pushed the umbrella stroller she was supposed to be sitting in all the way back home.

'Is Marco not interested, Gian?' Kit asked as they walked behind the little girl, in no particular hurry.

She couldn't imagine consigning her own child permanently to someone else's care, even if it was a doting Italian grandmother. But, then, a child of her own would come as such a precious and yearned-for gift to her, while Marco hadn't planned on becoming a father.

'I'm not sure,' Gian answered. 'And I don't think he is either. He's barely seen her. A couple of days when she first came into his life and he was still completely overwhelmed, and one visit since. It all happened very fast, and we did the expedient thing.'

'Yes, that's the impression I got from Aunt Helen.'

'Mum stepped in as soon as she found out. Marco's not uncaring, and he's not a bad person. But he is ambitious.

We've only now stopped to catch our breath, I think, and have realised that a more permanent decision has to be made. He could get sent to Europe or America in the next couple of years. If he's going to have Bonnie with him, he has to do it soon.'

'If he doesn't ever have her... Your mother will be nearly eighty by the time Bonnie is grown up.'

'I know. I'm very aware of the fact. I'm not sure that Marco is. He has no idea just how exhausting caring for a toddler can be. When he talks about taking her...' Gian stopped and shook his head, and Kit felt a pang inside her.

'Would he really do that?' Somehow, as soon as she really thought about it, she hated the idea. 'It would break your mother's heart!'

'I know, but I can't let her kill herself. She had a check-up last week.'

'Your idea?'

'You could say that,' he drawled. 'I had to drive her to the doctor!'

'But she's all right?'

'Her blood pressure's high. Her bone density isn't as good as I'd like, and I'm concerned about osteoporosis.'

'You don't *want* Bonnie to go to Marco, do you?'

'No,' he answered heavily. 'I don't. But the decision isn't up to me.'

'It's up to Marco, and your mother.' Kit understood. 'She's terrific, Gian. She'll handle it.' She'd dropped any pretence of objectivity now. She couldn't imagine how Freddie would let Bonnie go. 'Different from my parents. I admire her so much. Mum and Dad are great. Happy together, totally supportive of me and my choices. But they work hard in their business—they have a news agency on the Gold Coast, I can't remember if I've told you that—

and I think they'd throw up their hands in horror if they were left to raise another child at their age.'

Mention of her parents deflected Gian's attention. 'What do they know about you and James?' he asked.

'Just that we split up and I was unhappy for a while. I didn't tell them very much. I didn't particularly want my father up on a murder charge!' Gian laughed at this, and Kit spread her hands. 'What can I say? I'm an only daughter.'

He put his arm around her. 'You're great.'

She leaned her head on his shoulder, utterly happy for the moment yet knowing in the back of her mind that this was a stolen pleasure she'd pay for in the future with her heart's blood.

They had sandwiches for lunch, and then Bonnie fell asleep in front of a 'Wiggles' video. Kit sat beside her while Gian put away the lunch things. One minute she was thinking, Yes, 'Rock-a-bye Your Bear' is a sleepy sort of song, and the next, she'd drifted off herself. She'd slept so badly last night, thinking about Belinda and Travis Carter, their new baby boy and Gian.

She awoke half an hour later to find him standing there, eyeing her with a quizzical expression.

'Sorry, did I wake you?' he said. 'I'd decided not to, but then I was afraid that Bonnie might roll over and slip off the couch. I was trying to work out whether I could wedge her in place with cushions, without disturbing you.'

Bonnie was sprawled on her back, with her head in Kit's lap. 'I won't let her fall,' she said.

'You can't stay there until she wakes up.'

'I can.' She grinned up at him. 'It's nice.'

Too nice, in some ways. A sleeping child was so innocent and trusting and precious. She could hear Bonnie's steady breathing and feel the rhythmic movement of her little torso each time her lungs filled. Her black lashes were as long as Gian's, and her mouth was sweet and full.

Kit didn't quite succeed in enjoying this just for the brief interlude that it was. The sweet warmth she felt contained also, inevitably, a thread of loss. Her own, and a concern for Freddie's potential heartache that she had no right to feel.

When Bonnie woke again, she wanted to draw, then she wanted an afternoon snack, then she wanted to read stories, then she wanted to run around and around the couch and jump up and down on Gian's bed.

'This place is too poky, Gian,' Kit said, only half joking, even though it had good-sized and well-lit rooms, and a private, paved courtyard with a gas barbecue in it and a border of easy-care shrubs. 'You need a farm!'

They ordered Chinese food to go from a restaurant just around the corner, then they packed up Bonnie's things and delivered her and the Chinese food out to Freddie on the farm at six-thirty. Gian was brief and to the point in his mother's kitchen as he unpacked the hot containers.

'Bonnie likes fried rice. You like honey prawns, Mum, and you both like spring rolls. Kit and I are eating the rest of the dishes back at my place.'

'You're desperate to get out of here. Has Bonnie been that exhausting?'

'No, she's been lovely, but now we have other things to do.' His firm tone did not invite further questions, and if Freddie would have liked to ask a few, once again she didn't let it show.

Back in town, they ate Szechuan beef and Singapore noodles and hot chilli chicken at the little table in Gian's kitchen, washed down by Glen Aran white wine.

'Scrummy,' Gian said.

They hadn't touched for hours. Not since this morning.

It was as if they'd been afraid to, daunted by the prospect of having to keep what they felt in check until Bonnie had gone.

Even now that they were alone, there was an odd reluctance. They hardly talked as they ate, but Gian stretched across the table and took Kit's hand, caressing it with slow, seductive intent. He lifted it to his lips, kissed her knuckles and her fingertips and her palm. She couldn't even look at him at first, couldn't finish her meal, although her plate was still half-filled.

Finally, she managed to lift her eyes to his face, a little frightened about how much she must be showing of what she felt.

'Let's go to bed,' he said.

It took them quite a while to get that far. He pulled her to her feet, bending to kiss her as soon as she was within reach. The tastes of spice and wine were still on his lips, but they soon disappeared to leave only the taste of him. His warmth rose around Kit like a cloud, and she let herself sway almost weightlessly in his strong arms.

They both recognised the importance of taking this slowly, and of leaving no room for memories of anyone else. This was them. This was now. And it was important.

Gian couldn't dismiss the past straight away. He discovered in himself a need to cradle Kit's heart and her soul as well as her body. He knew he must do nothing to hurt her tonight, at the risk of fatally damaging the fragile connection.

Funny, he'd felt that way about Ciara for years—hyperconcerned not to hurt her. He'd been aware, always, of the six-year gap in their ages, and of the fact that she'd been still a teenager when they'd first met. As a male relative, albeit a very distant one, a second cousin, he'd felt the weight of responsibility. He'd acted on a presumption of innocence in Ciara which had turned out to be quite wrong.

This time, more mature himself, he knew he wasn't misreading the nature of the woman in his arms tonight. Innocence wasn't the word. Fragility certainly wasn't. Their connection was fragile, yes, but Kit herself wasn't. He didn't know the right word for the state of her heart, but there was something.

'Is this OK?' he asked, when they reached his room and he began to pull her simple blue knit top over her head. 'Tell me if it's not all right. Stop me if—'

She laughed, and pressed her fingertips to his lips, tilted her head a little. 'Hey,' she said softly, 'I've done this before, you know.'

'Not with me,' he growled back, anchoring his hands on her hips. 'Remember that, Kit.' The distinction was crucial and, despite what she'd just said, they both knew it.

'No,' she whispered. 'Not with you.'

It was different. It was so different, Gian found.

Kit had perfect skin, fine-pored and ivory-hued, with enough flesh beneath to make every inch of her feel soft and giving and wonderful. Her eyes were heavy-lidded with desire, but it was held inside her like the coals of a mature fire, quieter and stiller than leaping flames, but much, much hotter.

Every time he touched her, every place he touched her, he could feel the way sensation arrowed to her depths, and her hands on his body seemed to map every contour of his skin as if it was crucial for her to know him and commit him to memory.

When they were both naked, he felt his impatience building and his senses clamouring to complete their journey, but he guessed that she wasn't ready, and made himself wait. A window of stillness opened around them. He felt her hands rest on his body, and she pulled back.

'You should know,' she began, and those familiar spots of pink were back on her cheeks, give-aways to the strength of her emotion, 'when I found out that James was sleeping with Tammy, I had some tests. AIDS. Chlamydia.'

'Hell, Kit! You had to deal with that, too?'

She shook her head. 'I did it out of anger, not good sense. I don't think, now, that Tammy had been sleeping around, but for a while, oh, I *wanted* to believe that she did.' She gave a bitter laugh, then added, 'At least it's something I can offer to you now as security.'

'I wouldn't have asked for it,' he told her. 'But I'll offer the same. You won't pick up anything from this that you don't want.'

What about pregnancy?

The issue opened in front of him like a black hole. Kit had her head pillowed in the curve of his neck. She was saying something. Apologising for having brought up the issue of disease, and her past. He kissed her apology away, but hardly heard it.

He'd spent years reading about the psychology of infertility, and knew that sex and pregnancy would be inextricably connected in Kit's heart, twisted together yet pulling her apart. The desperate hope that had her thinking, month after month, 'Maybe this time...' It was such a hard habit to break.

And he didn't know what to do. He still had a heap of little packets strewn in the untidy drawer of his bedside table—leftovers from his marriage. Should he leave them there and forget about them? he wondered. Or reach across and pull one out? His need to keep from hurting her was so powerful that it paralysed him until Kit herself somehow sensed his distraction.

'Hey!' she said again, in that same soft, teasing tone she'd used before. She was smiling, displaying her need for him shamelessly. 'Get with the programme, Gian.'

Kit's mouth shaped the words like a kiss, and he groaned. Her fingers rippled down the six-pack of muscles that webbed across his lower stomach. They trespassed even lower, and he was lost, forgot everything but his own body, and her.

She reached for him, pulling him to the bed, and he let himself slide on top of her, stroking her breasts, supping stolen kisses from her mouth.

'Gian,' she breathed. 'Oh, Gian.'

Her eyes drifted shut, and he kissed her creamy lids, feeling the tickle of her lashes against his lips. She spread her limbs, ready for him, wanting him, and he surged into her, half his senses shutting down and the rest so powerful and sensitive that he and Kit were both caught at once, and didn't come to earth again until their need was fully spent.

'Hello,' she said, after a lengthy, sleepy silence.

'Hello,' he whispered back.

'Feeling nice?'

'Yes.'

'Mmm, yes,' she agreed, and smiled.

He kissed her, overwhelmed, and his foggy brain told him, I have to make this work. I have to. I can't stuff it up. Or let her push me away.

He could have lain there for another hour, replete and incredibly happy, and for a few minutes it seemed as if she wanted to as well. She looked dreamy, contented and still. It was a shock, jerking him to attention, when her muscles suddenly tightened.

Tangled around her, he could feel it at once, but before he could speak she pulled away, twisted, sat up and said heavily, 'I'm hungry. I never finished. There's more Chinese, isn't there?'

'Plenty. Heat it up in the microwave. The plates won't break.' He added much more urgently, 'Kit?'

Too late.

She grabbed a bundle of clothes—half of them his, he suspected—and walked out of the room, her body pale and curvy and graceful, even in her agitation, and he was left wondering, *Did I miss something? What suddenly changed?*

In the kitchen, Kit heaped spicy sauce and chunks of meat onto a fresh pile of rice on a clean plate and stuck it in the microwave. She didn't care what she was eating, and hadn't turned on the kitchen light. The light from the microwave brightened the room, and the apparatus hummed as her supper circled around and around inside it.

I remember, she thought. *I remember all the nights when I lay in bed afterwards, hoping a miracle was happening inside my body. Too afraid even to move, in case I ruined it. Putting a pillow under my hips and lying still for an hour, just in case, just to give it the best chance.*

Her dates weren't hard to track, and she knew she was mid-cycle. If there was any possibility that she was fertile, now would be the time. Which meant two weeks of that familiar, destructive waiting. Two weeks of helpless, exhausting battling against a hope that, despite everything, she could never quite kill.

Maybe this time…

She'd almost run from Gian's room, fleeing that traitorous hope. Dressing quickly in the bathroom, she discovered that she'd brought his socks and his shirt with her by mistake, and had left her bra behind. Her long-sleeved knit top was too thin and too close-fitting. She knew even without looking down that her nipples were still hard from the moist, delectable friction of Gian's mouth.

A moment later, she felt rather than heard his footsteps behind her. She turned reluctantly. He was barefoot and bare-chested, wearing jeans which he'd zipped but hadn't yet buttoned at the top. The waistband was peeling apart a little, so that the jeans rode low on his hips, showing the contrast of his olive skin against the black elastic of his briefs, and a fine line of dark hair that pointed downwards like an arrow.

His semi-nakedness was almost brutally male, powerful, sensual and totally unapologetic. He wanted to remind her—wanted to *confront* her—with the reality of what they'd just shared. He wanted her to remember the way she'd touched him in the most intimate places, and the way his muscles had bound around her, tightening convulsively as his climax came. Awareness and need coiled inside her again.

The microwave pinged, and they both ignored it.

'What happened?' he said.

She couldn't tell him, couldn't make it more real by putting it into words.

I was running away from the stupid, impossible hope that I might be pregnant.

'It's OK now,' she answered instead. 'I just…panicked a bit.'

'About what?'

She closed her eyes. 'Work it out.' Opened them again. 'Or don't.'

Actually, she didn't want him to.

'It's not— I don't want to make a big deal out of it,' she said quickly. 'I feel good. It's OK.'

'Hell, Kit.' He leaned closer, put his arms around her, knitted his fingers together in the small of her back and pulled her to him. Her breasts in their thin covering of knit fabric pressed against his chest and she felt the instant hardening at their peaks. 'Is it that hard for you to talk about?'

She stiffened against him, looked up into his face and he read the astonished question in her eyes.

'You told me to work it out,' he reminded her, light and gentle. 'We didn't use contraception just now. I deal with this stuff, remember? You're hoping. Or you're trying not to hope. Or you're just hating the fact that you're thinking about it at all.'

'Oh, Gian…'

He just held her. She listened to his heartbeat with her ear against his chest, then lifted her fingers to trace the contours of his pectoral muscles and the texture of his skin and hair. His tiny nipple was hard. He drew in a hiss of breath when she touched it, and didn't seem to breathe at all when she plunged her hand lower and let it hover and come to rest just inside the open waistband of his jeans.

She felt his cheek press against her temple as he bent his head to search for her mouth, and she met him halfway. It was a sweet, tender kiss. Their mouths parted softly, joined more deeply.

His fingers brushed her breasts through her top and she knew he could feel their hardened peaks. Without a bra beneath, the thin, stretchy fabric of the wool blend heightened her awareness of his touch and they both wanted more.

'This time…' he said. 'This time, nothing's going to hurt you. We'll make sure this stays purely about us and about now.'

And when, a little later, he reached to open the drawer beside his bed and pulled out a contraceptive, she didn't try to stop him.

CHAPTER NINE

NOPE.

She wasn't pregnant.

There had been just that one time when Gian and Kit hadn't used contraception, and yet she'd still not been able to kill the hope. She'd told herself that she had killed it, that she wasn't hoping, but as soon as she saw the evidence of her body's shift into the next phase of its cycle she knew she had been kidding herself. She'd been there before.

Nope, no pregnancy this time. Yup, she was bleeding with all the familiar heaviness and pain.

Stupid, stupid, stupid.

She had a lump in her throat and a stone in her gut.

Stupid.

Wanting a baby with a man she'd been fully involved with for so short a time, just because she was so in the habit of wanting a baby that she couldn't stop.

They were supposed to see each other tonight. She should have considered the fact that this phase would probably be happening by now, and shouldn't have made the arrangement. She couldn't see him when she was feeling like this. She didn't want him to see, to try and talk her out of it, or to tell her that it shouldn't hit her like this.

Kit was at work, in the delivery suite bathroom, in the middle of a shift and due to go off at three. She hadn't seen Gian here today, but that didn't mean he wouldn't have reason to show up at some point. She didn't want to talk to him, not in person or on the phone, but if she phoned his office and left a message with his front desk, she could maximise her odds of avoiding both. Not stopping to re-think, she reached for the phone.

'Just let him know, please, that Kit McConnell has had to cancel for today and will phone him next week,' she told his receptionist, hiding behind a very business-like tone.

She was working in the unit both days of the weekend, and in the hours when she was free, Aunt Helen always had plenty for her to help with around the farm. The re-mainder of the day, as well as Saturday and Sunday, passed as she'd hoped, with happy, problem-free deliveries at work and plenty of distractions on the home front.

'Rick Steele dropped in today,' Helen told her when she got home at three-thirty on Sunday afternoon. 'He wanted to know if I'd be interested in renting him part of the farm.'

'More vines?'

'Yes. The winery's doing so well he's been buying grapes from other growers this season. He wants to plant some new varieties next year but he doesn't have any acre-age left.'

'What did you say to him?'

'I told him I'd have to talk to Jim Rowntree.'

'Jim?' The Rowntrees owned the land adjoining this farm on the opposite side from the Di Luzios. 'What does he have to do with it?'

'He's been interested in the three westerly paddocks for a while, but he hasn't wanted the land east of the house, and that was no use to me. I either have to farm on a proper scale, or not farm at all. I'm not running a handful of sheep on a quarter of a piece of land. It just doesn't make sense.'

'But if Rick Steele wants the land to the east...' Kit started to understand.

'Exactly. It solves the problem. I've looked at the finances. The rental income, on top of what Brian had put away, will be enough. To be honest, Kit...' She sighed. 'It might be a relief to let go. Mike's flat out, helping me whenever he can, and managing his own place at the same time. When Sarah and I see each other, there's always too much to do. I'd like to be able to help her more with the children. And you've been doing so much, too. You won't want to do it, or to live here, forever.'

'I've been enjoying it. I've needed it.'

'Not forever,' Aunt Helen repeated. 'I couldn't give it up straight away, after Brian died. And I want to stay in the house for a good few years, yet. I didn't want to turn my back on all we'd built together on our land, he and I, all the happiness...the joys and the sorrows...that we'd had. But I think I'm ready, now.'

I'm not, Kit thought.

She didn't have the acceptance that her aunt had, and she could see and feel the difference. Aunt Helen showed a quiet certainty in her voice and in the look on her face. She'd been through the hell of losing her life partner, but she was over the worst of it and ready to seize hold of all the good things that remained—her bond with her daughter and her grandchildren, the chance to travel and to strengthen other family ties that were important to her. She was looking forward, not back.

But I can't.

She couldn't let go of wanting a baby. She couldn't let go of mourning the loss of hope.

Kit and Gian had spent a passionate two weeks since their first night together. Helen and Freddie must have suspected, even if they hadn't known for certain what was happening. Kit never stayed the whole night at Gian's unit in town, but several times she came home to the farm suspiciously late, having earlier told her aunt, 'I don't know when I'll be getting in, so don't wait up for me.'

Their encounters, each time, had been intense. Snatching interludes out of every rare window in their busy days when they were both free, they'd focused purely on the present. Making love. Seeing a movie. Driving to some secluded spot. As if by unworded agreement, they hadn't talked about those big, important words that ought to be written with a capital letter. Their Relationship. The Future. They'd talked a lot of nonsense, in fact, while Kit pretended to herself that she wasn't keeping track of dates, and Gian pretended -

Something.

Kit didn't know what, but there was something. There was a lot going on inside his head and he wasn't talking about any of it. The pattern was too familiar—a surface of happiness and laughter, while underneath hidden cauldrons of emotion bubbled. This was how it had been with James, far too often.

Their love-making was very different, though. Kit couldn't even remember, now, if that area had once been a success in her relationship with James. It must have been, surely, at first! But for several years it had been so completely overshadowed by issues of timing and goals, overshadowed by the baby that never came. It hadn't been a pleasure at all.

She felt her heart give a sick-making lurch when she considered the prospect of herself and Gian quickly descending to that same point, and could find nothing with which to reassure herself that it wouldn't happen.

Meanwhile, every time the phone rang in the kitchen at the farm, she flinched, wondering if it would be Gian, and every time it wasn't him, the knots in her stomach grew a

little tighter and thicker. She'd expected a quicker and more
impatient response, on his part, to her cancelling of last
week's plans.

'Trying to trick myself again,' Kit realised. 'Trying to
pretend I'm feeling one thing when really I'm eaten up with
feeling the exact opposite. I've done this before…'

Kit wouldn't know how many times he'd reached for the
phone intending to call her, Gian knew. She wouldn't know
how many times he'd had to coach himself out of it.

Wait. Give her a few days, then handle it in the Sicilian
way and make her an offer she couldn't refuse. He had a
lot on his plate at the moment. Marco would be in New
Zealand for two days on a business trip at the end of the
week, and Gian had finally persuaded him to take a detour
on the way back to Hong Kong in order to spend a few
days at the farm.

'We need to talk about this face to face,' he'd told his
younger brother, after another unsatisfactory conversation
by phone. 'And you need to see Bonnie. I won't handle it
at a distance. I won't let you make a decision that affects
all of us so deeply without your having spent at least a bit
of time with her. I'm not going to bulldoze you into anything, either. It's all too important.'

The prospect of Marco's visit put Gian on edge. The two
of them got on well, but Marco needed a little prodding at
times. Professionally, he was hard-headed, imaginative and
forward-looking, but in his personal life he tended not to
see the consequences of his actions as perceptively as he
might. There could be some tension and some awkward
moments when they talked about Bonnie's future face to
face.

Meanwhile, Megan Ciancio's theoretical due date would
arrive early next week, and he'd scheduled her for a

Caesarean this coming Friday. Appearing in his office in her wheel-chair for a final pre-natal appointment, she seemed as relaxed and confident as could be expected, and so did her husband Joe.

Gian was grateful for their faith in him, although somewhat paradoxically, he didn't want to tell them so, in case this hinted at the fact that he was well aware of potential problems, and thus knocked their faith on the head. Megan's lower torso had been thoroughly messed up by her accident, and he couldn't be sure that even a scheduled Caesarean would go smoothly.

'I want you to check in on Thursday evening so we can keep a good eye on you overnight,' he told Megan. 'And we'll deliver the baby first thing in the morning.'

'We're getting pretty excited about it, aren't we, Joe?' she smiled. 'Thursday's just three days away!'

Gian had arranged to take Tuesday off. Since Pete Croft's return to Glenfallon, after the time he'd spent in Sydney gaining extra diplomas in Obstetrics and Neonatology, he had more opportunities to adjust his schedule. He was confident of Pete's abilities, and he and Pete had agreed that they were an asset to each other, as well as to the town.

Gian had held his breath in the weeks following Pete and Claire's second separation. Would Pete crack and agree to move permanently to Sydney? This was one of the things that Claire insisted she wanted, having claimed at one stage that it would solve all their problems. Gian was certain, however, that the issues between them ran much deeper than that. A move wouldn't solve anything, particularly when Pete himself didn't want it. Selfishly, Gian didn't want it, either.

Pete had settled in at Emma Burns' house during her

absence. He had the girls to visit on a regular basis, while Claire dithered over her own future, and he was looking a lot happier.

Gian recognised an increasing need for a similar resolution in his own life, and had to curb the destructive impatience that he recognised in himself.

Wait. Don't confront Kit yet.

He hadn't phoned her on the weekend. It was Monday afternoon, and he wasn't going to phone her now. He would ambush her tomorrow, instead, in front of his mother and Kit's aunt so that she wouldn't dare to say no, and they'd spend some of those jewel-like hours together in which neither of them had time to wonder how possible any of this was, because it was happening, vivid and tactile and dazzling between them, then and there, and therefore it had to be possible.

'Kit!' Aunt Helen called along the corridor.

Having just brushed her teeth, Kit turned off the tap and called back, 'In the bathroom.'

'Gian and Freddie and Bonnie are here.'

'Oh. OK. I'll be out in a minute.'

Emerging from the bathroom, she encountered her aunt and they both said at the same time, 'You didn't tell me they were coming.'

They laughed, and Aunt Helen said, 'All right. Then it's clear. They didn't tell either of us that they were coming.'

'Collecting eggs? Not all three of them...' It was only around eight-thirty in the morning.

'No, dear,' Aunt Helen said. 'They seem to be under the impression that they're collecting you!'

'Oh. Right,' she answered weakly. 'Perhaps there's some arrangement that I forgot.'

She knew it was deliberate on Gian's part the moment she stepped into the kitchen and saw his face.

'Ready?' he said, shamelessly cool. 'We're a bit early.' His gaze locked with hers, a wicked looking glint in his eye.

I dare you to call my bluff, his face said.

'Just remind me where we're going,' she murmured. 'And tell me if I should bring a hat.'

'Definitely bring a hat. We're driving to Yerrinda.' Kit knew the town slightly. It was about an hour and a half's drive away. 'Dad's sister lives there, and Mum hasn't seen her for ages. We're dropping her off, and taking ourselves and Bonnie for a picnic. We'll pick Mum up again mid-afternoon, doubtless get invited in for afternoon tea, and get back to the farm at around six.'

'You're right. I'll need my hat.'

Helen walked Freddie and Bonnie out to the hen run, because even when she'd been told she couldn't actually have the eggs today, the little girl still wanted to collect them and put them in Helen's fridge. With the two older women safely out of earshot, Kit added, 'Why did you spring this on me?'

'Tactical manoeuvre. Sicilian style. An offer you couldn't refuse. I didn't want to give you time to think up a reason to say no.'

'I wouldn't have said no, Gian.'

'You cancelled last week,' he pointed out. 'Via my front desk.'

'Bad day, and I didn't want to inflict it on you. Nor,' she added ruthlessly, 'did I want to hear you trying to convince me that you could shake me out of it.'

'That about evens the score then, I think,' he answered lightly. 'Neither of us gave the other one a chance.'

Kit didn't know quite how to interpret the comment, so she carefully didn't try.

Bonnie had found her eggs. Six today—a lovely, exciting number, and three of them were unusually beautiful, a warm pinkish brown, covered in little white freckles. After a quick wash, they looked quite irresistible, and Bonnie reneged completely on her promise that she wouldn't mind the eggs going in Mrs Campbell's fridge instead of coming home to Nonna's.

She cried. Loudly.

'Oh, dear!' Aunt Helen said helplessly. 'They are particularly perfect, lovely eggs today, aren't they, Bonnie?' She looked at the other adults. 'Is this a tantrum? Am I not supposed to give in to it, or she'll think that's always the way to get what she wants? Freddie, help! I need the eggs for a cake I've promised to the fund-raiser at Sarah's kids' school, and I have to make it this morning, because Sarah's dropping in on her way home from town this afternoon.'

'Oh, goodness!' Freddie sighed. 'Marco used to have terrible tantrums as a toddler. I had the energy for them, then. Whereas now… Bonnie, don't cry, love. We'll get more eggs another day.'

But Bonnie roared.

'How many eggs do you need for the cake, Helen?' Gian asked.

'Four.'

'And there are six. Bonnie, love, listen. Do you want these eggs because they're so pretty?'

Her howls diminished rapidly as she listened. Gian had crouched down to her level as he always did when talking to her about something particularly important.

Eggs, for example.

She nodded at his words.

'Then how about you choose the two very prettiest eggs to have for your very own breakfast tomorrow, and Mrs Campbell will mind them in her fridge for you until we get back from our picnic?'

Bonnie nodded again. 'Choose.'

'Yes, you choose. One, two, OK? Two eggs.'

Bonnie chose the two brownest, speckliest eggs and Gian ripped the soft cardboard carton in half across the middle and showed her exactly how he was putting her eggs in one half of the carton and Mrs Campbell's eggs in the other half, so that they wouldn't get mixed up. Bonnie was perfectly happy about the whole thing.

'Bless you!' Freddie said in a heart-felt aside to her son, and Helen was able to go back inside with her egg carton in one hand and Bonnie's egg carton in the other, without further protest.

Freddie insisted on sitting in the back seat with Bonnie during the drive to Yerrinda. 'So you and Gian can talk,' she told Kit.

They dutifully did so, covering such thrilling topics as the state of the crops they passed in various fields, the prospects for winter rainfall, and the competence of their local elected representatives. Gian spoke very earnestly on each issue, rather as he might have spoken to a visiting health department dignitary whom he had been ordered to entertain but with whom he had nothing in common.

Under cover of Freddie's absorption in singing songs with Bonnie in the back seat, Kit muttered to Gian, 'You're doing this on purpose, aren't you?'

'Sometimes Italian mothers need a firm hand,' he replied.

'So it's Freddie you're teasing with this, not me?'

'Mainly Freddie. Tell me why you cancelled the other day, Kit.'

'I did tell you.'

'You told me you were having a bad day, but not why.'

'It's finished now,' she answered firmly. 'Today, if you leave me alone about it, I'll have a good day.'

'Is that a promise?'

'Barring the unforeseen, yes.'

They delivered Freddie to her sister-in-law, a silver-haired and very Italian looking woman in her seventies, who was old-fashioned enough to wear only black in memory of the loved ones she'd lost. She greeted Freddie in what Kit knew must be broad Sicilian dialect.

'Mi piace viderti assai!'

Freddie hugged her and answered, 'E tu! Pare bene, Nina!'

Predictably, Gian and Kit were begged to stay for lunch, but Gian was cheerfully firm. 'Not on your life! We have a picnic in the car, and a little girl with energy to burn.'

'Assimiglia Marco,' Nina said to Freddie. They were both looking at Bonnie, who was jumping around on the ground like a playsuit-clad rabbit.

'Si, ma in charactere, assimiglia Gian,' Freddie replied.

'Did you pick up what they were saying?' Kit asked Gian as they slid into the car again.

'Nina says Bonnie looks like Marco, and Freddie says she's got my delightful personality.'

'Hm. "Delightful". Say that for me in Sicilian, Gian.'

'Can't.'

'She didn't say "delightful" did she?'

'No.' He grinned, unrepentant. 'She was ambiguous as to whether Bonnie's resemblance to me was a good or a bad thing. I chose to interpret it in my own way.'

'And is she right, do you think? Is Bonnie like you?'

'I haven't thought about it that way,' he answered, suddenly much more serious. 'Bonnie is just Bonnie.'

Kit craned around. 'She's asleep.'

'Mum tired her out for us with all that singing. We're going to a spot I know on the bank of the Murrumbidgee River. It's only a few minutes away. We'll park in the shade, leave the car windows open, put down our picnic rug and just lie on the grass for an hour until she wakes up.'

'A whole hour? Will she sleep that long?'

'I'm an optimist, Kit.'

He glanced across at her and smiled, and she thought, I can't let him go. What will happen to me if this ends? I love him. What do I need to do to keep him in my life? I can't relax about this, yet. He says he's an optimist. Am I?

Bonnie slept for an hour and a half. It was a perfect day—mild and sunny, as winter days along the Murrumbidgee so often were. Gian spread the thick tartan picnic blanket on the short green grass beneath a huge coolibah tree and they lay part in sunshine and part in shade while a breeze rustled the long, pointy leaves overhead and the river slipped silently past, the colour of milky, greenish-brown tea. Gian offered to continue his discourse on weather and politics, but Kit wouldn't let him.

'Then I'll have to kiss you instead,' he threatened.

'Gosh, I never thought I was letting myself in for something as dire as that,' she murmured, and nothing very sensible happened until Bonnie finally woke up.

She was tearful and grumpy for a few minutes, as usual, then she settled down, had a little explore along the riverbank with Kit and was ready to go back for lunch. Meanwhile, Gian had made a ring of big, smooth river stones and set a fire in the middle of it. The flames were leaping, bright orange and almost transparent in the sunlight, when Kit and Bonnie got back to the picnic spot, and there was a pungent smell of eucalyptus wood smoke in the clear air.

'Mm, what are we cooking?' Kit asked.

She'd imagined sandwiches and a thermos of boiling water for tea, but Gian already had a billy can with a wire handle sitting on a home-made grill, also wire, over the flames, and there was a styrofoam cooler sitting on the ground, out of reach of the fire's heat.

'Sausages and lamb chops and pineapple rings to grill,' he answered. 'And potatoes wrapped in foil, when we get some coals. Little potatoes, so they'll cook fast enough for Bonnie. Lamingtons for dessert, to go with tea. Lemon cordial for Bonnie. Cold water for all of us. Apples if we're still hungry.'

It was as good as it sounded, their appetites and their taste buds sharpened by the outdoors. The pineapple rings were hot and smoky and sweet, the lamb chops were tender, and the sausages, eaten wrapped inside a slice of bread with a splash of bright red tomato sauce, were a flashback to the simple satisfactions of childhood.

Kit helped Bonnie to scoop out the steaming, floury centre from her outwardly charred potato. The little girl ate her lamington on her own, ending up with a face covered in jam, vanilla sponge, and the chocolate and coconut coating that covered the cake.

She wiped a good part of the mess from her mouth onto her sleeve, and the way she then examined the resultant chocolate smear suggested that she might be planning to try and suck the sleeve clean. Mess would be everywhere within minutes. This was the point at which Gian discovered he'd forgotten to pack any napkins.

'No worries,' he decided, and tucked Bonnie under his arm, crouched by the water and splashed her face and hands until he was satisfied. She laughed, and wanted him to do it some more.

'Hm. Maybe later,' Gian said, and came back with her still under his arm, to finish his tea. 'Having a good time?' he asked Kit.

'Perfect,' she answered a little sleepily. 'I don't want it to end.'

'No,' he agreed, and not for the first time Kit had the dangerous, seductive thought that they could so easily be a family—a happy, functioning family—if Bonnie had been their child. The illusion was too easy, and wasn't right.

Cooking over an open fire took time. It was after three when Gian doused the remaining coals with water from the river, while Kit packed away the remnants of their meal. At Freddie's sister-in-law's, the two women were sitting on the back veranda of the farmhouse in a patch of sloping winter sunshine, drinking iced lemonade and eating sugary Italian biscuits.

Irrigated by water from the river, the farm was operated by Nina's two sons and their families now, and was mainly devoted to citrus fruit. The trees had glossy green leaves, and boughs weighed down with their ripening crop of lemons and Navel oranges.

The Guarino brothers kept pigs, as well. Gian took Bonnie for a walk to see the animals, while Kit was persuaded to stay on the veranda and 'keep us old women company.'

She regretted it at first. Watching Gian and Bonnie wandering off, hand in hand, Nina Guarino made some rather sharp comment in Sicilian, and Freddie replied equally rapidly in the same language. Kit had a strong suspicion that the rapid flow of their speech wasn't an accident. They didn't want to risk her catching a word—or a name?—that she might be able to guess or recognise. Did she hear the word 'Marco' in there somewhere? And 'Gian'? She wasn't sure.

Freddie wasn't the sort of person to exclude someone from a conversation by deliberately using another tongue, and Kit was a little surprised. Hurt, too. If the exchange in Sicilian was designed to make her feel that she was missing something important, it had worked. After a few more quick phrases, however, Freddie went back to English and spoke to Kit.

'I'm sorry, Kit. Gian would be angry if he knew we'd been talking this way.'

It was an oblique sort of comment. Not precisely an apology, and inadequate as an explanation. Kit was left with more unanswered questions than before. A cloud had passed over the day, like the clouds that were beginning to build in the west. Fluffy and innocuous at the moment, but bringing with them the possibility of darkness and change.

One of the clouds sailed over the sun, making the temperature drop on the sunny veranda at once. The sun came out again a few minutes later, but Kit was restless now, a little uncomfortable and ready to go home.

Freddie ceded the front seat to her once again, and claimed Bonnie for herself in the back. 'You look tired, love,' she told Kit, touching a concerned hand to her shoulder.'

'A little,' Kit agreed, softened by the older woman's warmth.

She dozed for a while in the car on the way back to Glenfallon, and only awoke when they turned into the farm track that led to Aunt Helen's place. So Gian was dropping her home? She'd hoped, without admitting it to herself, that they would spend the evening together, as well.

He must have seen something in her face, and explained, 'Bonnie's eggs, remember?'

'Oh, of course.'

'I'm hoping you might want to pick up a dress so we can go out. Do you fancy Kingsford Mill again? Just the two of us, this time.'

'That would be lovely.'

'Change at my place. Have a shower there, if you want to.'

Come to bed with me, Kit.

He didn't say it, but the words flamed in his eyes, heating her blood. This time, she only nodded, letting her face show what she felt and adding after a moment, 'Just give me a minute.'

Alone in her room, still able to hear Helen and Freddie and Bonnie talking in the kitchen, Kit felt flustered and absurdly happy, as light of heart as if tomorrow didn't exist. She took a swishy, calf-length midnight blue skirt out of her wardrobe and matched it with a stretchy, slightly off-the-shoulder black top.

She collected heeled shoes and filmy black stay-up stockings, a bit of make-up in a zippered bag and a hairbrush, and put everything into a paper carrier bag from Glenfallon's best boutique. She was ready for Gian in a few minutes. They dropped Freddie and Bonnie and the eggs at the Di Luzio farm and headed directly to Gian's unit in town.

He looked at his watch as soon as they got inside the door. 'We've got plenty of time,' he announced.

'For what?'

'What do you think? For anything. For being alone. For

being together.' He wrapped his arms around her, seductive and familiar at the same time. 'You smell of wood smoke, Kit. You need a shower.'

'That's just an excuse, isn't it?'

'Transparently.' His mouth brushed the tender skin below her ear. 'I want to cover every inch of your skin with soap lather, then run my hands down your body, helping the hot water to rinse it away.'

'You smell of wood smoke, too, Gian.'

'Good…'

They hardly made it out of the shower, staying beneath it, wet skin wrapped in wet skin, until the water turned tepid. Gian had one huge clean towel ready, and he wrapped both of them inside it so tightly that they stumbled and laughed their way to the bed, then tumbled beneath his thick down quilt to warm each other.

This took a long time, and conjured its usual complex magic inside Kit—happiness and pain, promise and terror, love and dread. Gian never said anything about it. They hadn't talked, hadn't confronted serious issues, since that first night nearly three weeks ago.

Kit was aware every time Gian reached into the drawer beside his bed for contraception. She felt the extra passion and urgency in the way he returned to kiss her, having been absent for the minimum possible time from her arms. He thought that this was enough, and for the moment it was, but she knew it couldn't be enough forever.

Deep down, she was waiting for the other shoe to drop.

'Kit, are you going to sleep?' he whispered.

'No,' she answered. 'Just thinking.'

'Tell me.'

'About how much I love this, and how good it feels.'

He kissed her, content with what she'd said, and he was

probably right to be. She was the one who needed to change, relax, let down her guard against her own feelings, not think so much.

'Going to get dressed up to go out?' he asked.

'Are you?'

'I'm going to watch you, first.'

And he did, the rogue!

He lay in bed, sprawled out, lazy and naked, except for a twist of sheet pulled across his hips. He smiled every time she caught his eye. His lids were heavy and creased, and his eyes were dark and soft—the eyes of a man who'd just made love with a woman he cared about, the eyes of a man watching that woman dress for him.

'You're beautiful, Kit,' he said, heavy-voiced, when she was ready.

You make me feel beautiful, she wanted to tell him, but for some reason the words got caught in her throat and wouldn't come.

CHAPTER TEN

THEIR meal at Kingsford Mill was wonderful. Gian knew the owner, and spent a few very earnest minutes in conference with him while Kit waited at the bar.

'All fixed up,' he told her, when he came back. 'They're going to do us a special tasting menu, with wines to match. That picnic today made me hungry.'

'It should have had the opposite effect, shouldn't it? We ate pretty well at the picnic,' she reminded him.

'Too long ago.'

A succession of beautifully presented miniature courses began to arrive, and two hours swam by in a swirl of tasting, laughter and wine. Finally, they arrived at coffee and a selection of bite-sized petit fours. Kit was too sated even to speak.

Gian wasn't. He leaned forward, defying etiquette with his strong forearm resting squarely on the table, and said something that took her completely by surprise.

'Did James ever ask you to marry him?'

She felt as if she was riding in an express lift to a high floor, and it had left her stomach behind on the ground. 'No, he didn't.' Could have stopped there. Should have stopped there. 'He didn't believe marriage was necessary, or important.'

'Did you agree?' Gian watched her face closely.

She hated this subject—James, their relationship—and didn't want to go into the details.

'It hurt just as much when we broke up,' she said. 'But in some ways, it was easier. I'd have felt... royally conned by him… if I'd had to endure a divorce as well. So on the whole—' She tried a cool smile, but it wobbled, so she pressed her lips together to keep it in place. '—I guess that's one thing that James and I still agree about. Marriage wasn't necessary. It actually helped that we'd pretended living together was the same, when we split up and I discovered that living together wasn't the same at all. Can we drop it now, Gian?'

'Sure,' he growled. 'Finish your coffee.'

'I—can't.'

The meal was no longer ambrosial. Instead, it sat in her stomach as if it had taken up permanent residence there.

Gian was silent for what seemed like too long. She didn't know just how she'd ruined the mood, but somehow she had. His fault. Why had he asked about James? The bad memories his question had brought up shattered her determined illusion that she and Gian could keep on living for the present, the way they'd been doing.

They couldn't.

'Then we'll leave,' he said at last.

'No, you finish. I'm happy to watch.' She tried to make it into a suggestive reference to the way they'd watched each other dressing tonight, but it didn't work. She had that cloud-crossing-the-sun feeling again, only much worse than it had been this afternoon.

'I don't want any more, either,' he said.

Until they'd left the restaurant and were on their way to Gian's car, their comments to each other skated across the surface of emotion like a dragonfly darting across a pond. Gian pressed the button on his key fob and his car doors unlocked as the vehicle gave a whooping sound, as obedient as a dog.

He came to the passenger door to open it for her, then stopped so that she ended up in the subtle wash of his body heat, surrounded on all sides by car and man. She felt the familiar shape of him, close against her, but knew he didn't want to turn her into his arms. He was too angry for that, in a slow-burning way that almost frightened her.

'I'm not James, Kit,' he said, his tone dark and knotted with frustration. 'Get that straight. I'm not James.'

'You brought him into the conversation,' she answered. 'I didn't.'

'You didn't need to. For you, he was already there.'

'No, that's not true. I wasn't thinking about him at all. Not then.'

'Perhaps I'm being unfair. Making complications when they're not necessary. The mood was ruined, though, wasn't it?'

'Do we have to back-date it? We've had a fabulous evening, and a perfect day. Haven't we? Wasn't it enough?'

He responded to the urgency of her demand with a slow, and almost bitter smile. 'I guess I really am an optimist,' he said. 'Because I'd hoped for even more. Shall I take you home?'

'Yes,' she said, defeated and confused. 'I think we're both too tired to go on with this tonight.'

He kissed her in his car, in the yard outside Aunt Helen's back door, with only the sleeping hens as witnesses. The kiss was sweet, coffee-flavoured and long enough to melt her bones, but the disappointment of the 'even more' he'd hoped for had settled on her own shoulders now, as well, and she knew she'd failed him and frustrated him somehow.

'I'm going to be pretty busy over the next few days,' he told her, sitting back in the driver's seat with his hands locked behind his head. 'Marco gets here on Friday night.'

'I won't phone you, then, or expect to hear from you.'

He hesitated for a moment, then shook his head. 'You probably won't, no.'

'Thanks, Gian, for the meal.' It seemed very inadequate. She kept feeling that the evening wasn't supposed to end like this.

'Next week,' he promised her. 'We'll see each other. And we'll talk. In the meantime, perhaps this gives us both a chance to ask ourselves what we really want from this, what's possible, and where we want it to go.'

'Yes,' she answered uncertainly. 'I suppose it does.'

'We need that, Kit. I was wrong to hope for more tonight. I can see that now.'

'Oh. OK. I—OK,' she answered lamely.

He drove away as soon as she'd reached the back steps.

In the early hours of the morning, Kit awoke from a dream that immediately fled from her memory, leaving a new understanding deposited in her mind, whole and complete, like one of Bonnie's beloved fresh laid eggs.

He was going to ask me to marry him tonight, and I blew it, and in the end he was glad.

All those bitter things I said about James changed Gian's mind. Why didn't I see it?

Sleep evaporated completely, and she lay there till dawn, aching with regret.

I blew it. If I'd kept my mouth shut…

Would that really have helped?

She didn't know.

Megan Ciancio checked into the unit at just after five on Thursday afternoon, earlier than they were expecting her, in her wheelchair, and on the wrong side of the building.

'There's a reason for that,' she said. 'This baby doesn't

like Dr Di Luzio's timetable. I don't think I'm going to be waiting until tomorrow for a Caesarean. I'm in labour now!'

'Take Room One, just here on the left, Megan,' Jane Cameron said. 'Kit, I'll assign her to you. How are you feeling, Megan? Anything we should know about?'

'Well, the contractions aren't coming that often. Only about every fifteen minutes, but when they do, they're pretty intense, really pushing on my spine, even though the baby still feels very high. Dr Di Luzio said it might be like this, because I'm not quite the right shape down there, after the accident. That's why he won't let me try for a vaginal delivery, and it's why we didn't hang around at home for too long.'

'We'll phone him straight away,' Jane told her. 'You're in the wheelchair. Is that more comfortable for you?'

'No, it's worse. But I knew I wouldn't manage the walk. The past couple of weeks, it's been really tough. I'm so big, and I just don't have the strength or the control. I'm really just concerned for the baby, that it's being squeezed too hard, or something.' Her voice fogged.

As Megan's husband pushed her wheel-chair into Room One, Kit saw that she was shaking and sweaty, and asked her, 'Are you feeling all right between contractions, Megan? No other symptoms?'

'Awful headache. It's getting worse, actually. Things are starting to look blurry. Is—is that normal?'

'Let's check you out and see.' Kit was concerned, although she didn't betray the fact.

Megan had brought a nightgown and slippers, and Joe Ciancio helped her into them. She went to the bathroom, and then got as comfortable as she could on the bed. As soon as she was ready, Kit took her temperature, pulse and blood pressure. The first two were fine, but her blood pressure was too high, and almost at danger level.

Quickly, Kit felt the position of the baby and listened to
its heart. As Megan had said, it was high and seemed a
little oddly positioned, although it was head down. The
baby's heart rate was fast and strong, but as she listened,
Megan had a contraction, knifing pain through her body
and making the heart rate dip perceptibly.

'Let's see where Dr Di Luzio's up to,' Kit said, staying
calm. This should be all right. There were some problem
signs, but Gian hadn't expected this to be straightforward,
and Megan and Joe had very sensibly come in early. Early
enough? She hoped so, fervently.

She went back out to the nurses' station and found Jane.
'You reached him?'

'Yes, he's on his way.'

'Good, because her b.p.'s up pretty high, and she's right,
the baby doesn't like getting squeezed.'

'The obstetric theatre is free and ready for you, and
Clive's on his way, too,' Jane said. 'I wonder if he'll go
for a general. I know she wanted epidural. Different now
that this isn't the scheduled procedure she had booked for
tomorrow!'

'Babies have ideas of their own!'

Kit felt a rush of complicated relief when Gian arrived
and they met up outside Megan's door. He had time for a
brief smile, which she tried to return, then she quickly reported the dangerous blood pressure figures and he nodded.

'I wondered about that,' he said, resting his hand on the
door-frame and glancing into the room. 'It can be a problem
for paraplegic patients during labour. I didn't know how
Megan's system would respond, since her nerve damage is
only partial. Really hoped we wouldn't have to deal with
it.'

'Will she need general anaesthesia, so we can get the
baby out more quickly?'

'No, we'll go with the epidural, as planned, and that should bring it down.' His calm tone settled her own fears, until she saw the hard set of his face and the calculation in his narrowed eyes. He was sketching out scenarios in his mind, preparing for problems.

'You talked about nerve damage,' Kit said. 'But she's feeling a lot of pain in the contractions.'

'Doesn't surprise me. The pain's strong enough to overcome the lessened sensations. Her body's trying to do a job it's really not meant for, since the accident. I don't think we'd have a hope of getting this baby out vaginally. Let's get her into theatre, fast.' He strode into the room, dropping the frown from his face at once as he greeted Megan and her husband.

Within another minute, they were wheeling their patient along the corridor to the Obstetric Operating Theatre, where Clive was already waiting for them, as well as Juliet Woo, who would act as circulating nurse, and GP Alison Cairns, who'd handle the baby.

Megan was prepped quickly, while Joe hovered nearby, holding her hand whenever he could. Clive inserted the cannula for the epidural with efficiency and speed. The blood pressure figures had climbed even higher, and Kit was tense. If Megan began to convulse and lost consciousness... Megan and Joe remained unaware of the potential danger, although Megan's headache made her suffer badly.

'OK, Megan, can you feel this?' Clive finally asked, touching her foot with a cold surgical instrument.

'No, I can't feel anything.'

'Contraction coming,' Kit noted, and Megan couldn't feel that, either.

'This?' Clive persisted. 'Blood pressure figures dropping, by the way.'

'Nothing,' Megan said.

'And how about this?'

'No.'

'All yours, Gian. Starting to look nice, now.'

'Thanks.' His voice was as calm and controlled as ever, and Kit thought she was probably the only person present who realised he'd been far more concerned than he'd let on. She looked at his eyes above the mask he wore, hoping stupidly for the flash of his gaze in her direction, but it didn't come. 'Megan and Joe, you'll see your baby in just a few minutes, now.'

His hand was completely steady as he made the first incision, and he didn't look up again until he'd lifted the baby free. Standing close beside him, Kit was aware of every movement he made.

It was a darling little girl, around the seven and a half pound mark on the old scale. She cried vigorously at once, and had a healthy Apgar score at one minute, and again at five. She wasn't very pretty just yet. Her head was a little misshapen, her legs very bowed and her shoulders uneven after her last months of growth in Megan's abnormally shaped frame, but those things would correct themselves with time.

'Fantastic!' Gian said. The whole atmosphere in theatre was light and happy, now. 'I'm so pleased for you, Megan, and Joe.'

'It's great!' Megan's husband said. Like so many people in the area, he was of Italian origins, and still had a perceptible accent. He had an openly emotional Italian temperament, too, and didn't mind that people could see his freely flowing tears. 'Megan, you're a star.'

'What are you calling her?' Kit asked, as Alison Cairns laid the baby high on Megan's stomach. 'Do you know yet?'

'Dorina Alessandra. Dorie.' With her arms still strapped

to the table, Megan tried to kiss the baby, but couldn't quite reach. They'd be in Recovery together very soon, however. 'She's adorable! Oh, I love her!'

Gian's eyes met Kit's over their masks, and she wondered what he was thinking. He'd said they wouldn't be able to see each other until after Marco's visit, but she badly wanted to. And not like this, during a birth that might so easily have gone wrong. She just wanted a moment with him. Not long. Next week seemed too far away, when she didn't know what he was thinking and feeling, when she was so sure that she'd blown it badly the other night, and didn't know whether to confront him, or to let it pass.

Her own emotions had set into a desperate certainty that frightened her.

If he'd asked me to marry him, I would have said yes. Just closed my eyes to all my doubts and answered yes.

She didn't know how she could ever learn to let this man go, and yet she didn't have the answers as to how she could make love work. It was an impossible situation, and the only way she could see to resolve it, to even have a chance, was to talk to him, and to ask him about the other night.

She got her chance to see him a little over half an hour later, when Megan was in Recovery under Juliet's care, and Kit herself could take a snatched break. She'd brought some left-over quiche from home to heat in the unit's microwave for her evening meal, and wanted a cup of coffee to go with it. She'd just set the microwave going when Gian entered.

'Would you like some tea or coffee?' she said to him at once, snatching at the opportunity she'd thought she wouldn't have for days longer. He'd headed for the sink and picked up a glass from the draining basket, but a quick glass of water wouldn't keep him here for long enough.

He hesitated for a moment, then said, 'Coffee would be good.'

Clearly, he knew she wanted to talk. Circling back to the kitchen door, he eased it towards the jamb with his foot, so that it protected their privacy a little but didn't signal to anyone who might enter that they'd interrupted something important. Kit busied herself with mugs and boiling water.

'OK, Kit, shoot,' Gian said. 'This isn't the ideal place for a private talk, is it, so we'd better—'

'I know,' she agreed. 'Better get on with it.' She put a tea-bag in one mug and instant coffee granules in the other, and the microwave gave several metallic pips, announcing that her quiche was hot. She ignored it. 'You were going to ask me to marry you last night, weren't you? And I—' She gave a sharp little laugh, although it wasn't funny. 'I totally blew it.'

There was a beat of silence, then he said slowly, 'I think we both did.'

'How did we do that? Oh, I blew it because I didn't understand. But how did you?'

'I'm in love with you, Kit.' Perhaps he was, but he didn't make any attempt to touch her. It was a declaration that came with contingencies attached, not happy ever afters, and she didn't want contingencies, any more. 'And I think you're in love with me,' he went on.

'Gian—'

'It would have been very convenient if we'd agreed to get married as well, but what if it isn't enough? If love and even marriage aren't enough. I can tell you that I don't mind if we don't have a baby, and it's true. I'd rather have you. But to you it still matters. What you said the other night proved it. You're still so afraid that your own feelings about it would blow us apart eventually, and I realised last night that I couldn't promise you that you were wrong.'

'No, but—'

'So I didn't ask, after all.'

They seemed like the bleakest words she'd ever heard, and a huge part of her wanted to wrap her arms around the familiar strength of his body, look up into his dark eyes and say, 'No, but I don't care. I'll take the risk. Please. Ask. Right now. Ask, Gian, and I'll say yes.'

There was a problem with this, though.

He was right.

Somehow in the way they felt they'd passed the point of no return, but nothing else had changed. He saw the tears welling in her eyes and stepped forward, ready to kick that useful door the final six inches towards the jamb, take her into his arms and kiss her till the tears dried away, but she shook her head and whispered, 'Go away. It's all right. I'm not going to sob on your shoulder. I just need to think. About a lot of things. You've got Marco coming tomorrow, and it's late.'

He nodded, then reached into his back pocket and pulled out a clean, folded handkerchief. 'Dry your eyes. I want this handkerchief back next week'

She laughed through her tears. 'Starched and ironed?'

'Still salty and wet, for all I care. I just want it back.'

She understood. This was his way of saying, 'This isn't finished yet.' She would have paid dearly for a little of the same casual arrogance, right now.

'Look at her, Marco, can you really give her up?' Gian said. 'You have to be sure about this. More sure than you've ever been about anything in your life.'

Bonnie sat in her favourite swing in the playground near Gian's unit, laughing in delight as Marco pushed her higher and higher. Gian stood beside his younger brother, watching the two of them. In particular, he watched Marco's reaction to the crucial question.

'I don't have to give her up, do I?' Marco said, his expression torn between a smile and a frown. 'You'll always be my brother. I can see her whenever I want.'

'It's not the same. Think ahead. If you only see her once a year, she can't call you Dad. Do you want to be Dad, or do you want to be Uncle Marco?'

'You can't mean you wouldn't tell her!' Marco dropped his hands from the swing, and Bonnie twisted around to see why she wasn't going so high any more. Gian stepped closer, and took over.

'That she's adopted, yes,' he said, as he pushed. 'As soon as she's old enough to start to understand—and that's only a few months away.'

'I guess it is.' Marco looked at his daughter and frowned.

His behaviour with her was tentative and uncertain. He didn't know much about children, and had been quite startled to find how she'd grown and changed in the many months since he'd seen her. Understandably, she was wary of him, sensing his ill-ease, and they wouldn't succeed in forming a meaningful bond during such a short visit.

'But I'm not telling her who her biological father is until she's old enough to understand that,' Gian went on. 'And that point is a lot further away. I'm conservative, Marco, in certain areas. I have a reputation for it. If you sign those papers, she's calling me Dad, and I want you to think about whether you can live with that. You may marry, and settle back in Australia eventually. Or maybe somewhere else. If you send for her in five years, or ten, she's not going. If we agree on this, and I've adopted her, she's staying with me.'

'I'm not sure why the decision has to be made now.

Things have been working fine with the arrangement we've got,' Marco said.

'Tell that to Mum on a bad day! She's getting more and more tired, and Bonnie's getting harder to manage. Mum loves her to pieces, and she'd never give her up willingly. But you're her father. If you decide that you want her with you, Mum won't stand in your way.'

'Are you trying to argue me into this decision, or out of it? A moment ago, you were asking if I could stand to give her up!'

'I just want you to spend some time with Bonnie, and think through what you really want, and what's best for everyone. One way or another, a permanent, workable decision has to be made.'

'Bonnie has to come first,' Marco said firmly. 'That much I do know.'

Gian agreed with all his heart, but he didn't say so.

'Have you come for eggs?' Kit asked.

Gian had just driven into the yard, with Bonnie strapped in her seat in the back of his car. It was eight-thirty on a Friday morning, eight days after the birth of Megan Ciancio's baby girl, and Aunt Helen was cleaning the bathroom at the far end of the house. Wearing jeans and a light sweater, Kit had washed the breakfast dishes and prepared a lamb casserole for tonight. Gian should surely have been at work, but he wore clothes as casual as her own.

'No,' he answered her. 'I've come for my handkerchief.'

'Oh.'

'But I'm sure Bonnie wants eggs, too.'

'I'll grab a carton and come out with you. And I'll—The handkerchief is—'

'Forget the handkerchief,' he growled.

'Now you want me to forget it.' She was tense and on

edge, after days that had dragged with painful slowness. She'd known he wanted to see her once his brother's visit was over, but still had no idea what he would suggest about their future. The phantom marriage proposal that he'd never made hung in the air between them like a ghost. Even thought he hadn't said it, it had changed things.

'You know it's not important,' he answered her. 'You know it was purely an excuse. I want to talk.' He took Bonnie's hand and walked towards the hen run. Kit walked beside him. 'I've got some news,' he said.

For some reason, her heart started to pound. The news was significant, she could tell from his tone. 'Yes?'

'I'm adopting Bonnie.'

She gasped. This wasn't what she'd been expecting, although what she had been expecting she couldn't have said. 'Adopting her?' she echoed foolishly. 'Formally? Legally?'

'Yes.' He looked at her, his eyes steady on her face. 'Marco has agreed, and Mum's happy, and we've talked to a lawyer. It shouldn't take long to finalise. I've been thinking of this as a solution to the whole issue for a while, but didn't want to say anything until Marco had been here, and until we'd fully talked through what it meant.'

'That's... that's wonderful, Gian!' It left her head spinning.

They reached the hen run and Kit opened the gate with half-numb, clumsy fingers to let Bonnie inside. Bonnie was very good about not frightening the hens, now, and always went quietly and carefully, knowing exactly which tricky hen hiding places to check.

Gian and Kit both watched the little girl in silence for a moment—Kit with her brain feeling as if it was stuffed with the wool from Aunt Helen's sheep—then Gian wrapped an arm around her body and pulled her against him.

'So,' he said in an odd tone. 'There you go. Now I can

say it, at last. You wanted us to be able to have a child, and now we've got one. Marriage, as soon as we can arrange it. Instant family. Problem solved.'

His dark eyes glittered. There was anger and challenge in them, radiating out at her with powerful force, and his body contact wasn't warm and gentle, it was imperious and hard.

Kit remembered his pinpoint-accurate understanding of how she'd felt the night they first slept together, and the way he'd started using contraception after that first time, so that she didn't have to suffer through the on-going agony of faint, false hope. Today, he seemed like a different person, and the understanding she'd come to rely on had gone.

He couldn't be serious! He couldn't seriously suggest that darling little Bonnie was nothing more than a final, convenient peg to slot into the intricate puzzle of their relationship. That would be disastrous and wrong. For all of them.

She pulled sharply out of his arms. 'That's crazy!' she said, and her voice was shaking.

She pressed her fingers to her temples, struggling for the right words. There was a breeze today, sharp and cold and strong, and she felt a chill ripple down her spine.

'Bonnie's herself,' she went on. 'She's not something you can reach out and grab, to solve a problem, like a— like a surgical dressing on a wound. She's a unique, gorgeous little person, and I love her, and if you're adopting her purely as some sort of cure-all for the impasse we've reached…!'

She blinked back tears of outrage and disappointment.

'No. I can't believe this, Gian!' she exclaimed. 'Bonnie's far too important and precious to be used as a substitute for some abstract, non-existent baby of our own! You couldn't think that way. And I absolutely couldn't!' She dragged her fingers down her face, bristling and distant and hardly able to look at him. 'It's impossible. And wrong!'

'Ah, hell, Kit, exactly!' he answered. There was a new light in his eyes, and it was blazing bright. 'You've said it. You've said everything I hoped you'd say. Oh, dear God, I'm so glad!' He stepped forward, and this time, when she felt his arms around her, she found that he was shaking.

'Don't,' she told him, not understanding. He'd never played games with her before, and surely this wasn't the time to start. What was this about?

'Of course I'm not adopting Bonnie as a substitute or a cure-all,' he said.

'Then—?'

'I'm adopting her because that's the best solution for Mum and Marco, and for Bonnie's own well-being and security. As far as I'm concerned, you take what life gives you and you turn it into something good.'

'Do you? Yes, that makes sense, but—'

'I'm sorry to have played devil's advocate like that.' His mouth brushed hers briefly, confusing her more than ever. 'But it was the only way I could think of to force the issue, to break the deadlock we've somehow got ourselves into.'

'I still don't understand, Gian.' Tears sprang into her eyes. 'Even though I want to. I want this to be OK.'

His arms tightened around her 'Bonnie could never be a substitute, and neither could you. I love you. You. Not just you-if-you-could-have-a-baby. Or you-as-long-as-we've-got-Bonnie-so-we-get-to-be-parents. I love you with no add-ons, and no reservations. And I want to marry you.'

'Why?' she blurted. 'Tell me why.'

'For all the reasons.'

'Tell me! You're the only one who can make this all right. I can't.'

'Because I love you now. Because I know I'm going to love you for the rest of our lives.'

'Oh… Oh!'

'Because I want the rest of the world to recognise what we have. Isn't that enough? I've been torturing myself over the past few days—weeks, probably—trying to come up with something that was enough, since love, for you, so clearly wasn't. But I've had to accept that there isn't anything more than love. There isn't anything better. There's just love. That's our best weapon for dealing with everything else that might come into our lives. Adjusting to life with Bonnie, pursuing fertility treatment, anything. And love is all I've got to offer, Kit. If that's still not enough—'

'Oh, Gian, it is enough!' she answered him shakily at last. 'I'd started to understand that myself, but I wasn't sure about you. When it's expressed like this and felt like this, you're right. Love is enough. Love is everything.'

'So will you marry me?'

'Yes, oh, yes!'

He touched her face and looked into her eyes. 'There's a lot to sort out. We'll live at the farm, if that's OK with you. Mum wants to swap with me and move into my unit in town. We'll juggle the arrangements for Bonnie's care between the three of us, and it's up to you whether you go on working full-time, or whether you cut down your hours. I'd support you in whatever you decide. And if you want to try some more treatment for a baby of our own, at some point, you know I understand what that involves, and that we'll handle it together, all the way.'

'Gian, that's too hard even to think about. I want to. Of course I do. But I'm scared, too.'

'There's time. No decisions on that till we're ready to make them. We'll make this work, Kit.'

'We will. For the rest of our lives. Oh, Gian, when you

promised me that, just now, everything else seemed to fade away.'

Kit lifted her hand to touch his face, and a kiss hung in the air between them like fairy dust.

It didn't happen.

'One two three twenty-six forty eggs!' Bonnie called out proudly.

'That many, sweetheart?' Kit answered, turning to her. She felt Gian give a shuddering sigh against her body, and the smile he gave to his little girl was turned upside down. He didn't particularly want to have to count eggs, right now.

There were five eggs in the open carton, which tilted dangerously in Bonnie's hands as she approached the gate. Gian let her out of the hen run and took the eggs quickly. Aunt Helen appeared in the kitchen doorway, at that moment, and came down the steps.

'Hello, Gian,' she said. He still had one arm around Kit, who was leaning into his shoulder with no desire ever to let him go, and when Helen saw this, she smiled and understood. 'Freddie's going to be over the moon,' she told them softly.

'I'm already there,' Kit answered in a wobbly voice. 'And loving it.'

'Bonnie, would you like to help me make a cake with some of those eggs?' Aunt Helen asked. 'I think it might be appreciated, in certain quarters, if I kept you busy for a while. A chocolate cake, maybe?'

'Choccy cake!' Bonnie said, and tried to pull the egg carton out of Gian's hands.

Helen came and rescued it, took Bonnie's hand and led her towards the house.

Gian didn't wait until they'd disappeared. He bent his

head closer before Bonnie had even reached the steps. 'Because she's going to have to get used to the sight of her new parents doing this very often, isn't she?' he said softly to Kit, and then his mouth came down on hers.

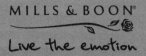

MILLS & BOON®

Live the emotion

Medical Romance™

FOR CHRISTMAS, FOR ALWAYS
by Caroline Anderson

When GP Katharine Crawford walks out of the shower in her hotel room and into the arms of the husband she hasn't seen in five years, they instantly rekindle the love and passion they shared. Drawn into Oliver's GP practice, and then his family Christmas, Kate feels happy and contented – until she reminds herself of the secret heartache that caused her to leave their marriage in the first place…

CONSULTANT IN CRISIS by Alison Roberts

Emergency consultant Neil Fletcher didn't expect to see Kelly Drummond ever again – let alone attend a Search and Rescue course with her. He's never been able to forget her. Working together to save lives, Kelly and Fletch now have to confront the truth about the past – and the secret Kelly has kept so long…

A VERY SPECIAL CHRISTMAS by Jessica Matthews

Practice nurse and single mum Claire Westin is more interested in treating patients than celebrating Christmas. But her gorgeous boss, senior physician Alex Ridgeway, is determined to remind her of its magic. He is convinced that bringing their families together will make every day of their lives special…

On sale 5th December 2003

Available at most branches of WHSmith, Tesco, Martins, Borders, Eason, Sainsbury's and all good paperback bookshops.

1103/03a

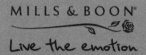

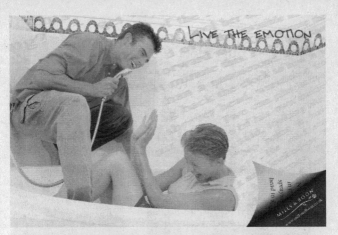

4 Books
and a surprise gift!

We would like to take this opportunity to thank you for reading this Mills & Boon® book by offering you the chance to take FOUR more specially selected titles from the Medical Romance™ series absolutely FREE! We're also making this offer to introduce you to the benefits of the Reader Service™ —

★ FREE home delivery
★ FREE gifts and competitions
★ FREE monthly Newsletter
★ Books available before they're in the shops
★ Exclusive Reader Service discount

Accepting these FREE books and gift places you under no obligation to buy; you may cancel at any time, even after receiving your free shipment. Simply complete your details below and return the entire page to the address below. *You don't even need a stamp!*

YES! Please send me 4 free Medical Romance books and a surprise gift. I understand that unless you hear from me, I will receive 6 superb new titles every month for just £2.60 each, postage and packing free. I am under no obligation to purchase any books and may cancel my subscription at any time. The free books and gift will be mine to keep in any case.

M3ZEF

Ms/Mrs/Miss/Mr ....Initials ....

BLOCK CAPITALS PLEASE

Surname..

Address..

....

....Postcode ....

Send this whole page to:
UK: The Reader Service, FREEPOST CN8I, Croydon, CR9 3WZ
EIRE: The Reader Service, PO Box 4546, Kilcock, County Kildare (stamp required)

Offer not valid to current Reader Service subscribers to this series. We reserve the right to refuse an application and applicants must be aged 18 years or over. Only one application per household. Terms and prices subject to change without notice. Offer expires 27th February 2004. As a result of this application, you may receive offers from Harlequin Mills & Boon and other carefully selected companies. If you would prefer not to share in this opportunity please write to The Data Manager at the address above.

Mills & Boon® is a registered trademark owned by Harlequin Mills & Boon Limited.
Medical Romance ™ is being used as a trademark.